FOR THE COLLECTIVE

D1603488

FOR THE COLLECTIVE

BY

CARMEN J. SPOONEMORE

L-Talia Publishing

For the Collective
Copyright © 2021 by Carmen J. Spoonemore
All rights reserved.

Cover images: Skyline © diversepixel;
silhouette © oOhyperblaster; licensed via Shutterstock.com

Cover design: Johannes Klein

Book design, cover formatting: Vladimir Verano, Vertvolta Design

Editor: Sirah Jarocki

Print ISBN: 978-1-7369729-0-8

ebook ISBN: 978-1-7369729-1-5

Published in the United States by

L-Talia Publishing, a division of L-Talia LLC
623 West Highland Drive, Seattle, WA, 98119

Contact: Publishing@L-Talia.com

Dedicated to my parents,
who taught me to live each day to the fullest.

Chapter 1

CUT

There is a moment in life when you leave childhood behind, or childhood leaves you. For me, that moment is now. I'm staring into my own fearful eyes. The small mirror in the corner of my compartment is rarely opened by the Collective— the act of looking at oneself is considered inherently selfish. Today, however, is special. It is the day of the Assignment. After today, we will no longer go to school. We took the Test yesterday, and the results direct what we do for the rest of our lives. Low scores get undesirable jobs; high scores get desirable jobs. The bottom five percent will be cut. The rarity of the mirror's opening adds to the finality of this moment.

I gaze at my reflection. Looking at myself makes me uncomfortable, and I wish I could return to the dream I had been having before I was clawed back to

1

reality by the brilliant lights of my compartment. Or was it a memory? Does the mere act of thinking of a dream turn it into a memory?

I close my eyes to avoid the mirror and focus on what I can remember. Faint music plays in my mind and an image slowly dances into view. A blurry, smiling face and a baby's laughter. I'm the laughing baby. My tiny arm reaches up and tugs on a piece of hair that is swinging in the warm breeze. The face says something, and it sounds distorted, as if it is trying to reach me from a great distance. I listen as hard as I can, straining at the vision, forcing it to become clearer. I think the voice is saying my name, but it pauses, as if refusing to let me hear. I'm laughing into the gently smiling face. Then, in an instant, everything changes. I try to leave, but the feeling clings to me, sucking me deeper. The smiling face disappears as a muffled voice yells something, and panic sets in. I can't see anyone but can feel the terror. I get passed from person to person. I start to cry. "Take the kid, get as far from here as you can . . . I'll hold them off for a while." Feet pound. I want to go back to the laughter. I want to go home. It's slipping away again, and I let it go. I rub my eyes to erase the vision.

I run my hand over freshly buzzed hair, perhaps in a subconscious effort to push the dream away. My hair. Some have no issue in controlling their selfishness. I, however, have always had an issue with vanity. When I was young, an instructor shaved my head in an attempt to eliminate my selfishness, a fate that many of us met.

Then the thin sheet of metal slides over the mirror telling me my time is up.

I am running behind, so I hurry to dress and put on my shoes. I do not want to be late, which would selfishly prevent others from proceeding. I stand in front of my door and wait for it to open. I hear a click and then a grinding as all the doors in the hall open simultaneously. I briefly make eye contact with the resident of the compartment across from mine before we both awkwardly look away. In unison, all my classmates and I step out of our compartments and start to walk along the hallway to the stairs. I glance behind me and see they are all stone-faced and jittery, as am I, facing forward and walking in time with the others. I find my friend Alex walking next to me. He looks terrified. He never studied or worked hard and was very disruptive in class, but he made everything more interesting and was nice to talk to. I was never well-liked by my peers. Alex, however, saw my predicament and took pity.

We all walk down the hall, the familiar rhythmic drumming of feet on the metal helps to calm my nerves. I fall in step with the others, and we file into our pod. The clear hovering vehicle lifts off and sails through the city. As we leave the student sector and fly deeper into the city, other pods join us. Some trundle along the ground on wheels. They're so slow that the clean new models in the sky pass them easily. Those who receive a poor assignment ride in the old models, dirty like them. I don't think I could bear the humiliation and embarrassment. The people in the highest-ranking jobs ride in the newest, cleanest pods.

The sun is shining, and as we ride, the warm rays are absorbed by the solar panels that line the roofs of all the buildings. We only get to leave the student sector for special occasions, so seeing the city is a special treat. As our pod hovers over the travelways, I watch the city speed past. A cluster of medium sized grayish buildings sits at the center of the Collective. The student sector is a similar grayish group of buildings with an education hall and small field in the middle. It's close to the edge of the Collective, although we do not have to endure the unsightly outer rim unless we receive one of the lowest assignments. I've never seen those inauspicious areas of the city myself, but I've heard of the dirt and grime that litter the streets and the smell of rust and decay that permeates the air. A large line of tall buildings purposely blocks the unsightly view from the rest of the Collective.

As we move closer to the center of the city the buildings get progressively smaller and more attractive until we come upon the meeting hall. The grand hall is next to the leaders' compound, which is elegant and pure white. White is the color all leaders and important affiliates wear. The leaders' compound is large and is shaped like the perimeter of a rectangle with a large courtyard in the middle. A short distance away is the building that serves as the leaders' dwelling, but this is obscured from the rest of us. The gathering hall is a half dome with seats that go several stories high. In the center, there's a stage which is where we will wait to be assigned. The whole ride took only a few minutes, but the tense atmosphere in the pod made it feel more like an hour.

Our pod docks, and we are ushered into a waiting room until the entire Collective is ready. My heart quickens, and my hands start to sweat. I nonchalantly dry them on my shirt, not wanting the others to see. I look around and see the others are also unconvincingly trying to hide their nerves.

We hear the beep, and the door opens. The eyes of the entire Collective are trained on us as we slowly walk in a line and climb onto the stage to find our seats. I watch as our leaders step forward. Only three of the four are present: Charles, a tall, dark-haired man with deep set brown eyes; Jenna, a short mouse-like woman who looks as though she hasn't had a decent night's sleep in months; and Elisabeth, the principal leader, with blond hair that is exclusively worn in a tight bun that exaggerates her already harsh features.

Elisabeth steps forward and addresses the Collective: "Welcome to the assignment of generation E24." The Collective politely claps until she motions for them to stop.

She continues: "Yesterday these students took their placement tests. Today they are adults, and we will now assign them to their proper positions. We will start with those unfortunate individuals who tested in the bottom five percent and who will be no help to the Collective. As we all know, they will be cut, seeing they have no further use."

As we watch, the hologram hovering in the air projects name after name. I watch breathlessly as they appear and the unlucky individuals are escorted out. Then Alex's name appears. He looks white with shock. Then, as if bracing himself to do something desperate, he stands up and runs towards the main entrance. For what purpose, I don't know. It isn't like he can escape the city without being caught. Even if he made it all the way to the outer edge and to Outside, there is nothing for him except for the toxic earth that is covered in nuclear waste and radiation. I see a guard raise his gun and point it at Alex. I look at my feet, not wanting to see the inevitable. I'm ashamed that he would do something so selfish. I hear the zip of the bullet and know that he is gone. Maybe it is best for the Collective that someone so selfish is gone. I am not really sure what happens to those who are cut, but I've always thought these worthless individuals might as well be dead. Yes, it is good that he is gone.

Chapter 2

ASSIGNMENT

Elisabeth pauses for a fraction of a moment, then continues, "We will continue with the job assignments. First, trash disposal personnel." I look at the projection hoping it's not me. Names appear. As I watch each go past, my heart begins to race. One by one, the newly assigned delivery personnel, construction workers, textile makers, caretakers, nurses, doctors, scientists, and many others leave their seats and stand with those who received the same assignment. Soon all the Assignments I've ever heard of have been given out. My hands start to sweat again as I wonder if there's been a mistake, but the Collective never makes mistakes. I'm the only one left. Then I hear Elisabeth announce, "Future Leader," and I see my name appear. The Collective turns to stare at me.

I rise, and the Collective begins to clap. After a minute, Elisabeth hushes them and instructs those of us who are newly Assigned to follow technicians who will be placing our chips, the final step to fully becoming productive members of the Collective.

•—•—•

"This may hurt a little," says the attendant behind me. I close my eyes, bracing myself, but all I feel is a slight pinch. "There," she says, "you can look now." I flick my eyes up to a mirror positioned so I can see the back of my neck. My head is strapped into the chair to prevent me from moving during the procedure. I see the skin on the back of my neck peeled up, held open by two metal prongs on either side. Strangely enough, it doesn't disgust me. Instead, it feels as though it's happening to someone else. I think that was the point of the pills they had us swallow before separating us up into these small white rooms. I watch the metal instruments deftly moving under the thick layer of muscles surrounding the spinal cord. A small black box is then delicately placed inside my neck. The shiny surface of the chip catches my eye, and I watch as tendrils slowly extend and burrow deep into the tissue.

"Can you lift your left arm for me?" I try to lift it, but it doesn't budge. I try to pull it up harder and harder until—smack—my arm shoots up, hitting the attendant. "Don't worry, happens all the time," she says, unfazed. I notice that my sudden motion also disrupted the mirror that had let me watch the procedure. I don't want to interrupt, so I sit in silence as the technician works.

She asks me to move different parts of my body and adjusts the placement until everything feels normal. I don't know how long it takes as my mind begins to drift. The glowing white walls send me into a stupor. Watching the procedure happening had been grounding, and without it, I drift further and further away.

She says something, and I don't quite make it out. She repeats it more slowly, and I know she wants me to wiggle my fingers. Why? What's wrong with my fingers? Do I even have fingers? What are fingers? My eyes drift down to short little sticks attached to my hand. Yes, these are fingers, but are they mine? Although it looks like they are, I can't feel them or move them. Ah, there they are! The little sticks wiggle. I laugh; how silly they look. Somewhere I hear a muffled voice saying something, but it's too far away to matter. I think someone else comes into the room, but I can't really tell. They walk around so they're facing me. I laugh again and say, stumbling over my words, "why is your face doing that?" It morphs like a bubble, suddenly swelling up. The tiny mouth slowly moves, and a voice says, "this is going to hurt." I laugh at how silly they look and wonder vaguely what's going to hurt. In a split second, I know what. A stinging pain floods the senses that have abruptly returned to my body. My leg randomly kicks as the attendant fiddles with the chip placement. I feel the sting of the cold air on the opened flesh, and something must be connecting because my vision blurs, then winks out, sending me further into a panic. Tears stream down my face.

Then, nothing.

"I'm sorry that had to happen, but we almost lost you," says Elisabeth. The attendant undoes the straps, freeing me from the metal frame. "Anyway, welcome back."

•—•—•

Whispers swirl around the pod, and I can feel eyes searing a hole into the back of my head as we ride back to my compartment. I don't look at them. They are all jealous. I know they are—me, who they so often ignored, not giving me a second thought. I still feel a bit nervous at their hostile stares, but I smile a little and look out the window. There is nothing they can do now. They all know I'm better than they are. Before we left the ceremony, the other leaders informed me that this would be my last ride back on this pod, and in the morning, my uniform and my new pod would pick me up. In the coming week, I will move into the compound where the leaders and other important officials reside.

The pod arrives at the dock and we disembark. As we walk up to our compartments, the rhythmic drumming of feet on metal is gone, replaced with a chaotic smattering of random footsteps. In the few hours since we left, everything has changed. We're all strangers now. The mutual respect we once held for one another is gone, and everyone knows who's better, who's smart, who's more selfless. Many are hanging back and staring at me. I walk faster to my compartment to get a reprieve from their piercing eyes. The door closes, and I can breathe. I close my eyes and lean my head against the cold wall. I can feel myself smiling. For years I studied all night for the Test in order to get a good Assignment, to not be cut, but that is all done with now. I remove my shoes, change into my sleeping clothing and lie in my bed waiting for 9:30 when my new chip will send a signal to my brain and I will fall asleep. I look at the clock and watch the minutes pass by, infinitely slowly. Finally, I am plunged into sleep.

Chapter 3

WHITE

I look around. I'm back in the gathering hall in front of the Collective and Elisabeth is looking at me, saying there has been a mistake. She says there was an issue with the results and that I am going to be cut. No, this can't be true! I did everything perfectly. I sit in shock, and a guard walks over and lifts me out of my seat. The Collective begins to laugh at me as I proceed to the doorway where the individuals that were cut had stood minutes before. I see the normally cool and collected leaders look pityingly at me before starting to laugh. I feel the shame rise within me and try to focus my eyes straight ahead. The Collective's laughter rips through my ears.

"Stop," I beg with them, "please stop," but they just laugh harder. I hang my head and stumble over my feet. The Collective laughs louder and louder. I scream at them to stop, then I lose all my energy, and my yelling turns to tears, drowning me in disbelief. No, I don't deserve this. I worked so hard. I am not just some toy to amuse the Collective, to be tossed away. I feel the heat building inside me as I turn to face the Collective. "No," I say watching them closely. I am indispensable, I will prove that to them. I will not be forgotten.

●—●—●

"We made the right decision, Elisabeth," says Charles as he looks over at her. "And such progress!"

"We will see. After all, this is only phase one," Elisabeth says shrewdly.

"True," says Charles, "we have gotten all the information we need for tonight."

He pushes the button to end the simulation.

●—●—●

I wake in the morning drenched in a cold sweat. It was just a dream. A strangely vivid detailed dream, but not like the one I usually get. I look around my compartment, reassuring myself that I have not been cut. Yes, there on the table is my new clothing—not the gray that signifies a student, but bright white.

I eagerly walk over to examine the spotless fabric, not caring that the metal floor is freezing my toes. I pick up the stack of clothing, inspecting it: clean cut white pants, a shirt, and a sweater. My fingers work their way along the stitches, marveling at the intricately woven wool. White, the color of a leader, of someone who matters, someone to be envied. I pull the shirt, then the sweater, over my head, then put on the pants. I quickly put on my shoes before consuming the gel-like goo the sustains our bodies. I'm excited, but I realize that I'll have to face the stares of those who live in this hallway as soon as I walk through the door. I linger in my compartment for as long as I can, dreading the next moments to come.

My door opens, and I move quickly, walking fast down the hall and trying to avoid the others. The unorganized mass of people moves to the loading bay. All different colors. Many hang their heads in shame, shrinking away from the patched dark clothing that signifies their irrelevance. Some have the decency to look away, but others bear looks of disdain. Some talk and laugh with others that got the same assignment. I duck my head and walk faster to my new pod. I enter the calm interior. The doors slowly close, and I feel my new life beginning, clothed in white.

Chapter 4

MALLORY

As the pod begins to move away from the dock, I look around and see a girl a few years older than I smiling and motioning for me to join her. I walk over to her and sit in one of the plush seats adjacent to hers. It looks like she's about to burst with excitement.

As soon as I sit down, she bursts out, "Hi, my name is Mallory, what's your name?"

"I—" I try to start talking, but she is already speaking. "I saw your assignment yesterday, don't worry, everyone reacts the same way, or at least I did. I don't know about anyone else anyways, when I was assigned Future Leader I had no idea what it was as there hadn't been one chosen recently, and I didn't expect it either. I mean I studied really hard just like everyone else, but I was thinking that doctor or architect would be super cool because, y'know, only people who score 100 on their test get considered to be a leader and even if you do score a 100 it's still very rare to get Future Leader like we did . . . ."

She trails off, noticing that I'm not following, "Oh sorry, of course you don't know. I'm just used to being the one that needs things explained to them because I'm the youngest, or was the youngest, I guess," she says smiling. "Anyway, how you get assigned Future Leader is kept very secret so people don't try to become a leader just because they want power because that would be selfish," she says seriously. "To get assigned Future Leader you first need to get a 100 on your test and ... well, I don't know the rest of the criteria. If they don't think you'll be good enough, you might get cut or reassigned, normally to a low-level assignment because most training for other assignments is over by that time."

I straighten up in my seat. I thought that once you were assigned it wasn't possible to be cut. My concern must be showing on my face because Mallory quickly proceeds, saying, "I'm sure you'll be great. I heard them talking about you before the Assignment. Especially Charles, he was very excited about you. Anyways, you don't talk much do you?" I open my mouth to respond, but she continues, "I didn't talk much before either, but at the compound where all of us live, people talk all the time, and there are loads of super important people too. The guard leader lives there and the head of education and, well, basically the head of anything important or anyone that really helps the Collective, and of course, the leaders Elisabeth, Charles, Jenna, and there is another one but I don't remember his name. He's gone all the time. I'm not sure where he goes, but anyways they all live there. It's a big switch from your old compartment. It was for me, but you'll get used to it soon enough," she says grinning.

I quickly interject before she can continue, "I talked a lot when I was younger, but the teacher became very strict as we grew older. I really only talked to my friend Alex."

"The Alex that tried running away after being cut? The Alex that was …." she trails off, her face twisted with something between sadness and regret.

"Yes," I say. "He joined school later than most, but everyone loved him. He was funny, clever, and kind. He was the only person who made an effort to talk to me." I pause, seeing Mallory's eyes getting wider and wider, so I hastily add, "but if I had known what he was capable of, I never would have even talked to him."

"You probably won't want to say that he was your friend in front of the others, they didn't take kindly to what he did. I think I could understand . . . . Oh, we're here! Are you excited? I was so excited for my first day of training."

"Sure" I say, unaccustomed to her enthusiasm.

"Don't worry, they really like you. I'm sure you'll be fine," she says as we walk out of the pod. It is raining and she's pulled her jacket over her head. She turns and walks towards a tall bright white building in the distance, "go to the front desk over there," she points to another white building, "you'll get your directions there."

I try to ask her what a "front desk" is, but she has already hurried out of ear shot. I turn towards the building she had indicated. The rain doesn't bother me much, but the others disembarking from the pod grumble unhappily and hold things over their heads.

I pull open one of the two large glass doors and walk into the "front desk" building. A long hall stretches out in front of me, illuminated with a soft white glow that emanates from the walls, ceiling, and floor. I look around, not knowing what I'm supposed to do now that I'm here. Someone else, a tall woman who is carrying a stack of slim electronic screens, pulls open the door. She starts to walk away, but I clear my throat to get her attention. Back in school, people were everywhere: people to help you find places, people to know where everyone should be going, people to constantly watch your every move. The abrupt change is unsettling, but that's one of the things the chip is supposed to help with. I had expected to already see overlaying directions on my vision, but nothing has appeared. I clear my throat. The woman turns, and I say, "sorry, but what's the front desk?" She laughs, "the front desk is right there." She gestures to a white box in the corner of the hallway. "Go inside, say your name, and your schedule will load," she says before continuing down the long hall.

I open the door to the box and step inside. I say my name and wait for something to happen. Nothing. I say my name again louder and still nothing happens. I assume it's broken, so I step out of the box. An itincrary appears before my eyes. I move my hand through it, and it disappears. I move my hand back and it reappears. I stare at the first box, and after a second, it expands so I can clearly read, "meeting with Charles." When I look down, I see that a blue arrow has appeared on the ground telling me where to go. I follow it down a hallway and around a corner to a door. It swings open revealing a grinning face.

"Good to see you found your way alright. I am Charles, I will be your mentor and one of your teachers until you are ready to become a leader."

Chapter 5

THE BOOK

Charles leads me down one hallway and then another until I suspect we are deep in the building. He turns a corner, and we are at a dead end. I look at him, puzzled, wondering why we came all this way to look at a wall. Just as I'm turning around, assuming he made a wrong turn somewhere, he continues walking straight ahead and puts his hand in the center of the wall and pushes. A rectangle of wall moves back, revealing a hidden room behind it. Charles smiles, "I love showing people that," he says as he walks into the room.

Unlike the rest of the building, this room's walls are covered with small colorful rectangles that are cramped onto ceiling-high shelves. In the center of the room, there's a small white table with several chairs on wheels. Charles walks along the walls looking for something and selects an auburn rectangle and brings it to the small table. He opens it in front of me and looks at me expectantly. I have no clue what I'm supposed to do.

"I'm sorry, I forgot to explain it. This is a book," he says. "A book is a primitive way to store information. Many years ago the leaders decided to collect all books and conceal them. The information within the books was deemed unsafe and would harm the Collective if it were released," he explains.

"Why didn't you digitize it? It seems like a security risk," I say.

"Yes, well, I prefer physical copies instead of digital. All of the leaders have access to this room, but I am the only one who uses it. Jenna would agree with you about the security risk, but I think it's worth it. Just look around," he spins in his chair, motioning to the tall walls lined with books.

"Yes, it's great, but how do they work?" I ask. He laughs. "Nothing special, it is just like the normal reading that you did in school—just physical instead of digital," he explains.

I look down and see writing on the book in large letters: *The Beginning of the End*. I tentatively brush my hand against the delicate pages. I start to read. The book tells a story about how the world ended. Not nuclear warfare, as I had been told all my life, but how a disease had wiped out the majority of the population, how fires, hurricanes, and rising sea levels killed off many more, leaving those remaining to survive on what remained of Earth. Within the conflict that ensued, two groups emerged: the Collective and the Outsiders. The Collective only wanted peace and tried to work with the Outsiders to come to a compromise, but they wouldn't listen. I look up at Charles, who had picked out another book and is leaning back in his chair with the words held up close to his face.

"Why wasn't I told this earlier?" I ask him. Charles puts his book down and leans forward conspiratorially.

"You learned in school that the biggest problem of our predecessors was nuclear warfare from the Outsiders. That's actually only partly true. We teach most people only the basics so they'll understand why the Collective is so important. It might cause a panic if everyone knew all the details. But the Outsiders were a serious threat. They attacked us again and again until the Collective had no choice but to take action," Charles explained. "Their selfishness nearly wiped out our species," Charles added grimly. "The world was broken, and we fixed it— now there is no disease, no hunger, and we all work to help each other instead of ourselves."

I continue to read the pages of the book as it describes the heroic actions of Generation A72. They subdued the Outsiders and tried to save as many as possible, getting many to join the Collective, thereby saving them from the horrible fate that they would have suffered. How idiotic and selfish must they have been to ignore the Collective's invitation to join? Charles explains that the Collective is still sending out those who get cut to clear bands of dangerous Outsiders that remain. A daunting and impossible task, he explains, as the fugitives who survived are the dirtiest and most unethical of all. They are the ones who will kill us all without a second thought if they have the chance. They must be stopped.

Chapter 6

I spend the ride back to my compartment ignoring Mallory's questions and think instead about what Charles told me. I can't understand why the Outsiders wouldn't want to join the Collective. How selfish must they be, how ignorant? Why would they try to fight the Collective instead of working for the greater good? Only caring about trivial, insignificant things that only benefit themselves—things that cause meaningless pain, suffering, and death. I understand the need for this information to be kept hidden from the Collective. If it were widely available, the outcome would be catastrophic. Only a few would be able to handle it. For many, the knowledge would be devastating. People might start to question the Collective, resulting in many selfish acts.

"Mallory?" I ask.

"Uh, finally, you've been ignoring me." She puts on a pout, but her affable smile pokes through after a second. "I was just thinking, has Charles shown you his room?" She asks.

"Oh yeah, he showed it to you too?"

Mallory nods. "Cool isn't it? He said I can go down there whenever I want to read. I spend most of my extra time down there," Mallory says.

"What have you learned?"

"Well, many of the books are about the same stuff. It just talks about how great the Collective is," she explains.

"Of course. What were you expecting?" I say.

She looks at me, puzzled. "Well, I already know how great the Collective is. What I don't know is what the Outsiders think of us. There's nothing about what happened from their perspective. And well, I think that to fully understand someone, you need to think like them, and to think like them, you need to know their motives. Without knowing the *why* behind someone's action, you can never understand them, never beat them."

We sit in silence for the rest of the ride.

Chapter 7

PLAN

Voices whisper.

"We don't have a choice."

"What do we do if we get caught?"

"We'll be fine. Remember, he said this is for the Collective."

"If we don't do it now, we will lose our opportunity. It has to be tonight. We'll be greatly rewarded for our heroic actions. We might even get reassigned."

Silence falls. The congregation had all received poor assignments and the tantalizing prospect of moving up in society is too difficult to resist.

"Don't forget to wait until the water starts so it muffs the sound."

"I don't know if I want to do this. It-it seems wrong."

A sound of shifting comes from around the room as all look at the dissenter.

"If you want to be selfish and not help the rest of the Collective, you can leave."

"OK, OK, you're right, sorry. For the Collective."

Others murmur it as well, and it bounces around the room. "For the Collective." The quiet shuffling of feet fills the room, signifying that everyone will do what must be done.

Chapter 8

SPIRALING

I sit alone in the pod. All the others had been dropped off at the leaders' compound or other compartments for high-ranking personnel, and I am the only one left. The pod stops in front of my old student compound, and I step off. It's my last night in my old building. Tomorrow I'll move into the leaders' compound. On my first day, Charles said they would have a room ready for me as soon as possible, but it's been almost a week. I head toward my compartment. Since there are lots of people on the main staircase, I walk around the side of the building to the back staircase to avoid them. As I'm walking up the stairs, I only run into a few people. They just ignore me, and I ignore them. I pull my compartment door shut and gather my shower supplies. Although it would be selfish to spend too much time on one's body, basic cleanliness is a necessity.

I walk down the back staircase to the basement where the communal showers are located and walk into the room. Immediately I know something is wrong. It's an unspoken rule to not look at others in the shower room, but everyone is looking at me. Not one to back down, I walk into an empty cubical and pull the curtain shut. I set my clothing on the dry shelf above the tap and turn on the water. I sigh as I feel it running down my back and the timer starts. Each shower runs for exactly five minutes in order to conserve water, thereby ensuring that there is enough for everyone. I let the warm water run over my face and neck. Right now, with the water pounding against my face, I can feel my muscles relaxing. I had not noticed how tense they have been. The stress from the past week is gathered in my neck, and I roll it to the side, loosening it even more. That's when I hear it. Shuffling and murmuring is coming from directly outside my cubicle. I can feel the dread welling within me like the water pooling at my feet. I grab the shower head in one hand and with the other, I tighten my grip on the slippery handle that changes the water temperature. I jerk the curtain open and see about twenty figures poised in front of me. Someone in the group shouts "now" and the room falls into darkness.

I hear scrambling, and at the same time, I turn the water as hot as it will go and point the nozzle at them. Screams echo around the dark room, and I know the water has found its mark. I feel a hand close around my wrist and pull; my grip instinctively reacts and the shower head drops to the floor. There is a split second in which I prepare to lunge for the nozzle, but the others have rushed forward while I hesitate.

A fist slams into my chest, and I stumble back, trying to regain my balance. A set of rough hands drags me forward into the fray. My eyes have adjusted to the dark enough to make out vague flailing figures crowding around me. More hands pummel my body, sending spikes of pain wherever they connect. I swing my fists wildly, trying to make these attackers back up. Two people grab my arms as someone else punches me in my throat. My lungs burn as I try to breathe, but it's like my lungs are trapped shut. I pull my wet arms from the grip of my assailants, and my hands fly to my throat as I gasp, trying to get air back into my lungs. For what seems like an eternity, I gasp, lungs burning for air. My eyes water from the war between my body and brain, until finally, I cough, and cool air rushes into my lungs. I am relieved that I'm not dead. That comfort passes when a particularly hard blow strikes me under my chin, sending me sprawling to the floor. A triumphant shriek echoes through the room, and I hurriedly try to stand, only to be immediately kicked back down. I try to fight back as much as I can, but pain is coursing through my veins. The crowd has gathered around me and booted feet are kicking as hard as they can. I kick back until someone restrains my legs; then I punch until someone grabs my arms. I thrash about, trying to get loose, until a hard blow to the head sends me spiraling into darkness.

• — • — •

"Why can't we see?" asks Elisabeth impatiently.

"I don't know," says Charles, puzzled, as he repeatedly pushes a green button.

"Did you even play the program? It won't work if you don't turn it on," scolds a voice.

"Yes, I did, Jenna. Something is wrong," says Charles.

"It always works. As long as neurons are firing, it should work," Jenna says. They look at each other.

"Pull up the cameras from the dock starting at the time the pod was arriving," Charles says, trying to contain his rising panic.

The screen flickers, then shows an image of a white pod with one future leader disembarking. "There," says Elisabeth, "now pull up the ones for the staircase."

"There's no one there," Jenna chimes in.

"Yes, we can see that, Jenna!" Charles says exasperatedly.

"Try the back staircase. That's where I would go when I was assigned future leader so I wouldn't draw attention to myself," says Jenna.

"That might be the first useful thing you have said today," huffs Charles.

"Thank you," Jenna says. Charles opens his mouth as if to say something, thinks better of it, and closes his mouth.

"There," says Elisabeth, who had been fixed to the screen not paying attention to their squabble. "Now change the camera to hallway three."

Everyone watches in tense silence, their eyes trained on the screen.

"There, right outside the showers." There is another long pause as nothing on the screen changes.

"Do we have any cameras on the inside?"

"Ew, Charles," Jenna says.

"Not like that. It's just nothing is happening on screen, and unless someone knows a different way out of the showers. . . ."

"Speed up the footage," Elisabeth says. Jenna walks to the comm and pushes Charles out of the way. She rapidly hits buttons until she is satisfied. All three stand back and watch as various figures enter and leave the shower room, blurred by the fast-forward. Nothing unusual happens, and eventually Charles says, "look at the time stamp. It's passed 9:30. Everyone's chip would have put them to sleep."

Jenna rewinds the footage and watches it play through again, making certain that they didn't miss anything. Once she is certain, she types on a keyboard before sitting down and leaning back.

"I hope I'm not bothering you, Jenna, but what are you doing?"

"Relax, Charles. I just sent a team to the showers in building F3," Jenna says. "It'll be fine," she says, sounding a little unsure but making a concerted effort to hide her trepidation.

Elisabeth nods and says, "send me a message as soon as you get an update," before walking out of the room.

Chapter 9

TOMORROW

I try to open my eyes, but one is swelled shut. I blink with the one that can open and try to sit up, unsure of where I am. My body objects and I groan as I lie back down.

"Ah, welcome back," says Charles with a relieved smile. "You had quite the eventful night."

"Yeah, I guess so," I try to say, but my voice comes out dry and raspy, not at all like my own.

"Do you know who did this to you?" Charles says seriously.

I try to think, but all I can remember is the pain. "I don't know. I'm sorry, but I . . ."

"No need to apologize. It is quite all right," Charles interrupts. "You will need to stay here for a few days, and I'm afraid your lessons must be postponed for the time being. Once you are well, you will be moved into the compound with the rest of us. It is heavily guarded; you will be safe there," says Charles.

I nod.

"We should also discuss the consequences for the guilty individuals. If you want, we could have a trial arranged."

A trial in the Collective is rare. Normally, everything is quietly and efficiently dealt with by the guards. But on special occasions where it can serve as a lesson to others in the Collective, guilty individuals are displayed in court. Perhaps it will be better for the Collective if it is made clear that certain actions result in a harsh fate. I consider the individuals who attacked me. I think they should face the embarrassment they deserve. I want them to be punished, to feel guilt, to know that they were wrong to have tried to hurt a future leader.

"Yes."

I try to sit up, but Charles stops me. "In due time. And they will receive their punishments. But for now, you focus on getting better."

•—•—•

I blink my eyes, and the shapes of Charles and Elisabeth appear in the corner of my vision. They are whispering about something. I wait for them to notice that I'm awake. Being too focused on their conversation, they don't seem to notice me. I clear my throat. With a start, they both look over. I pretend to yawn. Its not hard to pretend I didn't hear their conversation since only a few disjointed words were loud enough for me to hear. They walk over, and Elisabeth curtly asks, "Are you well enough to talk?" I nod. Her reputation precedes her: Elisabeth gets right down to business. Not being one for pleasantries, she despises wasting time and avoids doing so whenever possible.

"Charles has informed me that you wish to identify the individuals who attacked you. Is that correct?"

"Yes," I say. "Any with the level of selfishness that can drive them to violence must be cut."

"I quite agree," says Elisabeth. "The other leaders and I have formulated a plan to find and punish the guilty individuals. However, we will need your help to complete it, if you are willing."

She already knows my answer. A smile is already turning her lips when I say, "Yes, of course."

•—•—•

Two days have passed since I agreed to help Elisabeth with her plan. I lie waiting for everyone else to fall asleep. My chip will not put me to sleep tonight; it will keep me awake. Over the past few days, an attendant had covertly spread the information that I would be returning to the student compound while preparations for my new compartment were being made, which is true. What they don't know is that I'm here to update their chips with a recording feature to see who was involved in my attack. Hopefully the guilty individuals will discuss my return to the building and mention some names. I wait in the darkness until I get the notification that the others' sleep chips have been activated. The doors simultaneously open, and lights flicker on one by one, illuminating my way. I walk out of my compartment and enter the one across from mine. As I step into the room, I am conscious of every sound, every squeak, every shuffle and creak, even though there is no possibility of them waking.

I feel on edge, like something is wrong. I don't have the option to stop now; I've already agreed to do this, and I know the leaders will be very disappointed if I back down now. A solitary figure lies asleep on the bed in this compartment. I take a thin rectangular box and hold it so it's not quite touching the person's neck. Normally, all updates are sent out by the signals to everyone in the Collective, but this program is more direct and targeted for only those who could have hurt me. A blue light flashes beneath the skin, and I wait until it turns off before continuing down the hall and into the next compartments, trying to get to everyone. It's nearing dawn as I finish the last one. Tomorrow the chips will record all conversations. Tomorrow we will know whose heart is filled with selfishness, who is a danger to the Collective. Tomorrow we will find out who will be cut.

Chapter 10

THE TRIAL

Muttering swirls around the room. Elisabeth has gathered the Collective to pass judgment on the guilty individuals. We all know that this trial is purely a formality and is only to show the rest of the Collective what happens to those who work against its leaders. The attackers are standing in a line on the stage, facing the Collective.

"Why?" A single word that carries so much. We wait for one of the individuals to speak up.

"We were told to," one splutters.

"By whom?"

"I don't know," another says, looking to the ground. The Collective grumbles; we hate liars.

Elisabeth turns to face the Collective, "We have indisputable evidence that these individuals committed a heinous crime. They are here to be sentenced. Any who oppose this, speak now." No one in the Collective speaks up. Her part completed, Elisabeth sits down with a bored expression on her face and Charles stands.

"How do you plead?" asks Charles as each new individual approaches the stand. Most plead "guilty" and are led away. For those foolish enough to believe they have a chance, a brief trial is held where they are allowed to speak briefly in an effort to convince everyone that they were in the right before the Collective convicts them. Their excuses are flimsy, always resorting to receiving mysterious orders from an unknown source. I see their stupidity, thinking that they will be allowed to go free, rejoin the Collective, have all of this be forgotten. We would never let that happen.

At some point, Elisabeth grows impatient with the duration of the trial and requests that I give a testament to the Collective so things will move faster. I look over at Mallory and see she has not been able to look at the accused individuals; she knows their fate. No matter how hard they fight or what they say, they will never escape, and it breaks her heart. I, for one, only hope their suffering will continue after they are cut. None of them have the decency to look at me, but I stare at each one in turn, willing them to look into my eyes, to see that they have no future or hope, to see that they will be cut no matter how fervently they protest, to see that I am the one who determines their fates. I do this for the Collective.

Chapter 11

TEST

The cold breeze whips across my face, sending a prickling sensation down my spine. I clench my fist with overwhelming pride as I look down on them from the rooftop. The plan had worked: the chips recorded the conversations between two individuals naming everyone who had been involved in the plot. Over the whistling of the wind, I hear footsteps approaching.

"You did a good job," says Charles.

"Thank you."

I turn my head and am surprised to see Elisabeth standing behind me. I'm trying to puzzle out how long she has been there, but she interrupts my thoughts saying, "I came here to congratulate you, but it seems as though Charles has already done so." She abruptly turns and leaves. Charles gives me a warm smile, then follows

Elisabeth down the stairs. When the last of his footsteps finish echoing in the cement stairwell, I unclench my hand. The wind cools the sweat that has beaded on my palms, chilling my fingers. As the last individuals fade from view, it's like they are erased. The only thing that remains is my memory.

•—•—•

"It's easy if you focus!" scolds a nasally voice from across the table.

"I'm trying but it's hard," I reply, forcing down my frustration.

"Do I look like I care?" she responds. It doesn't. I'm in class with Jenna, although I'm not learning much. She's trying to teach me to program a chip. *Trying* being the operative word.

"You forget the connecting code. Again!" she says exasperatedly.

The next hours are agonizing. All I do is stare at the digital model of the chip that is spread across my vision and try to create a program while sitting in the middle of Jenna's office as she criticizes my work. I'm almost excited when I realize that it's nearly complete, but all of a sudden it's gone. The word *deleted* flickers in my vision, and I groan. I then spend 30 minutes listening to Jenna endlessly rant in her dreadfully annoying voice. I am finally able to reconstruct the deleted program, but it doesn't run.

Jenna has had enough and practically pushes me out of her office. She slams the door with a loud thud, and I open my schedule to see if I have her again tomorrow. Thankfully, I don't. Tomorrow I have a lesson with Elisabeth. It's the first lesson I'm going to have with her. I drag my feet all the way to the pod. Mallory is sitting in one corner, and I sit next to her with a sigh. She asks what happened and I tell her what a horrendous day I had. Mallory listens intently as I talk. She begins to look puzzled as I near the end of the story. She says that the same thing happened to her when she had her first lesson with Jenna.

"It could just be a coincidence," I suggest.

"I don't know how something so similar could happen to both of us," she says. "What if it's not actually learning how to program but something else?"

"Why would they do that?" I ask.

"To see how well we can function under pressure and how well we deal with failure . . . ."

"Like a test," I laugh at my own joke but she is still serious.

"I think you're right. It's a test to . . . to see if we'd make a good leader."

"Good thing we both passed then."

"Yeah," she says with a chuckle before spending the rest of the ride silent. I know what she's thinking—the only test we were supposed to take was the placement test. If that wasn't the last test, then what else is a test?

Chapter 12

COMPARTMENT

The pod pulls up to the leaders' compound. For so many years I had wondered what it looked like up close. It feels surreal. The large, sterile, slightly ominous building doesn't seem like a place where anyone would choose to spend their time, yet the others are happily filing out onto the grass surrounding the compound. My old building was not perfect, but it was comfortable and simple. In comparison, everything here is so extravagant. Instead of stark hallways, the main entrance here opens to a large, brightly-lit room where, in place of practical desks separated by dividers, there are a multitude of comfortable-looking couches and squishy armchairs as well as several communal tables where some are already seated. The buzz of lively conversation fills the room. Some leaders head over to the array of seats and benches to relax or continue their work while others cluster in groups to chat. The most astonishing thing, however, is the security. Silent sentries stand around the room and up into the stairwell. The light is absorbed by the black that adorns their uniforms, turning them into shadows.

I shake the unsettling feeling that the guards instill, eager to see my new compartment. It is much larger than the old one. In one corner there is a bench that mirrors the ones downstairs, plush with a pillow on either side. On the other side of the room there's a neatly made bed. A whole wardrobe is filled with my new pristine clothes, organized by season, but the most striking difference is the personal shower. Charles must have advocated for this, as I don't think many other compartments have the same thing. Even though this building has somewhat excessive security, it is still a relief to know that I won't be ambushed while getting clean ever again. I catch movement as I examine the shower compartment, and I whirl around. There's a large mirror fixed to the wall next to the shower, completely uncovered. I examine myself in it briefly, taking in the gleaming white of my clothing. I grin.

I walk back down the stairs and meet up with Mallory, who has been waiting in the comfy parlor room. We spend the evening here, talking about our lessons, what our Assignment was like, and what type of leaders we hope to be.

I watch as some people walk around with plates piled high with . . . something. "What is that?" I ask Mallory.

"Oh right. I forgot. That's food. The leaders and other important individuals eat this. It's really good. Put whatever you want on your plate then meet me in the corner," she says laughing.

I compare the colorful shapes and succulent smells with the tasteless goop I'm accustomed to. I pick up a plate and do as Mallory suggested, taking one of everything, then walk over to where she's sitting in a corner. "So basically you put it in your mouth and chew, careful not to go too fast or you'll make yourself sick. That's what happened to me the first time."

I put a piece of the food in my mouth and am shocked by the flavor and texture. Mallory laughs again at my expression. The hall slowly empties as everyone eats the food and retires to their compartments. As the clock hits 9:00, we say our goodbyes. I am so tired, and full, that I just fall into bed and wait for 9:30.

•—•—•

"The test today was very successful," Jenna says. "It was nearly impossible to get any reaction."

"That's good," Elisabeth says.

"Are we going to do a test tonight?" Charles asks.

"No, Oswald wanted to be here for the next test, but he is supervising the search of Outsiders."

"Ah, I see," says Charles, "have they had any luck?"

"Yes, they have found a camp in the woods. They are planning on raiding it tomorrow," Elisabeth says.

"How exciting," says Jenna. "Do we know how many are still out there?"

"Unfortunately, no," says Elisabeth, "but we will."

Chapter 13

OSWALD

The quiet of morning is interrupted by the boisterous voices of soldiers in a small clearing in the middle of the woods. Some sit finishing their morning "meal" while perched on rocks and fresh tree stumps. Some animated soldiers have begun dismantling the long row of small tents while they chat.

"SHUT UPPPP!" yells a voice from a much larger tent on the other side of the clearing. It is accompanied by an airborne pillow flying in the direction of the soldiers. Everyone falls silent.

"Oswald?" a soldier asks, entering the tent.

"What do you want?" asks a fatigued man from beneath a pile of pillows. He shoves the pillows from his head, revealing tired eyes and disheveled blond hair, and slips his feet into two plush slippers before standing.

"Well, did you come to tell me something or simply to irk me further?"

"No sir. The new soldiers have arrived."

"Finally," Oswald grunts, "tell them I'll be there in a minute."

The soldier turns to leave and the leader yells after him, "and tell them to be QUIET!" The soldier leaves and Oswald takes a long drink from a flask on a table before begrudgingly pulling on a Kevlar shirt and pants. He then splashes his face with water and spends roughly ten minutes fixing his hair before giving up on the tangled mess.

Oswald extravagantly flings open the fabric entrance of the tent and poses in front of the congregation. "My name is Oswald, and I am one of the leaders of the Collective. You all tried to attack a future leader, if I am not much mistaken." The front line of soldiers look down in embarrassment. He smirks, then starts laughing and struggles to get out the next sentence, "Oh, oh my, you really are stupid aren't you." The surrounding soldiers, taking a cue from Oswald, guffaw loudly. When he finally stops chortling, Oswald straightens. Everyone is instantly silent. "Alright here is what's gonna happen. We are going to raid a camp of Outsiders. Do all you can to take out all your teen angst on them. How's that sound? They're worthless. But if any want to join the Collective, then we'll let them. For now, anyway. Understand? Good." He chuckles to himself as he pivots and brusquely walks back into his tent.

The soldiers quickly obey, and soon they all lie hidden in bushes around the outskirts of a small village. Children laugh and run in between the small huts, but the cheerful chatter that fills the air turns to screams of terror which ring through the trees at the first gunshot fires. Soldiers hidden in the brush leap out, and the air is quickly filled with sharp whizzing noises and screams. Many of the Outsiders are struck and fall to the ground. Those who try to fight back are intercepted and killed by the new soldiers. Within a few minutes, it's over and the soldiers gather all the survivors at the center of the small village. There they are forced to kneel in a line, a gun pointed at each head.

Oswald ambles up to the end of the line and nudges a bleeding man with his foot. "Are you awake?" The man lets out a groan. "I'll take that as a yes," says Oswald. The rest of the soldiers laugh. Oswald continues, "Will you join the Collective and fight against selfishness?"

The kneeling captive spits on Oswald's shoes. "Never," he rasps. Oswald makes a pouty face and says, "are you sure?" The leader does not wait for an answer. He waves his hand lazily, like he's brushing away a fly. The crack of a gun cuts the morning air. "Alright, who's next," Oswald says rubbing his hands together. This continues down the line until a young boy says, "Yes."

"Don't do it, Owen," someone yells.

"Quiet, woman," Oswald snaps. "What was that child? You want to join the Collective?"

A small boy sits with tears slowly pooling in his eyes. Oswald crouches down and says to the boy, "Owen, is it?" The boy nods silently. "And you want to join the Collective and fight against selfishness?" The boy is crying harder now, but he nods. "Don't cry, rejoice! Welcome to the Collective, Owen." The soldiers begin clapping, and the child is led away from the small village. Oswald stands, "Who's next?"

Chapter 14

FLAWS

Mallory and I sit leaning against a tree in the late afternoon sun. The courtyard in the leaders' compound is strangely barren. The leaders had something to attend to today and couldn't train us. None of the others who normally lounge in the grassy field seem interested in us. Our only instruction was not to leave the compound. This seems to trouble Mallory.

"OK, but why? I mean, really, why can't we leave the compound?" she says.

"Huh?" I respond, caught by surprise.

"If we're going to be leaders, we at least need to know who we'll be leading so we can reflect their needs and wants in our leadership," she explains.

"Maybe they're just worried for our safety," I say halfheartedly.

"Don't you care? Does this really not bother you?"

Offended, I get up from my slump. "Of course I care, I just think about it differently. The leaders will decide when we leave the compound and when we become leaders. They know what's the best for the Collective. And soon we will too."

She looks at me flabbergasted. "What gives them the authority to decide what's best for the entire Collective? A good leader doesn't tell people what's best for them. I'm the only one who can decide what's best for myself, not others; same for you and for everyone. Do you ever think about what they want and need?"

"No, I guess I haven't. It just seems like the leaders do what they think is best," I weakly add.

"Yes, that is what they do, but we can lead differently. We can be more than the Collective's leaders; we could be leaders of the Collective. Am I making any sense right now?" Her eyes meet mine.

"Yes, you want to be a leader who represents the members of the Collective, not just someone who tells them what to do," I finally say, beginning to see her view.

"Exactly! Individual freedom."

"But Mallory, how will you keep control if you let them do whatever they want?"

"We'll inspire loyalty instead of getting it through intimidation and misinformation! We'll let each member choose what they want to do, to find their own passion. And I don't just want it to be me, I want us to work together to make the Collective the best it possibly can be!"

She sees what I don't, what no one else sees. She is selfless enough to see the flaws in the Collective, and she will be able to fix them. She will make the Collective achieve its fullest potential. *We* will make the Collective achieve its fullest potential. Together. She laughs and leans back against the tree. "Best not to tell the leaders, even though it's for the good of the Collective. I don't think they would necessarily agree. We should pretend to agree with their way of thinking until our time comes." I nod my head. I am much more confident than Mallory is that our current leaders wouldn't agree with her way of thinking.

Chapter 15

EQUAL

"To be taken seriously you must be direct and to the point," says Elisabeth. "Today I will give you a situation, and you will construct an appropriate response. The problem you will be addressing is this: there is a story circulating that an individual has found a way to work around the sleep component of the chip. What is your response?"

I work on an appropriate response for the problem, sketching out a few ideas and considering different outcomes for roughly an hour. Abruptly I realize the answer *she* wants. This is another test: she doesn't want me to make up a response. She wants me to do what she would do. Anything else would be unacceptable in her mind. Having realized this, I sit back and say, "nothing, you don't address it."

Elisabeth looks up from the screen she had been examining, seeming unsurprised. "And why is that?" she asks.

"If you address it, it makes it clear that it happened or is possible; if you don't address it, everyone will think that it was just a baseless rumor. If it is known that it is possible, others may attempt to work around the sleeping block, and that would cause a larger issue than the original problem. You say nothing, then you discreetly investigate who it is. Once the individual is found, you cut them by creating an excuse for the disappearance, and the whole problem goes away quietly."

Elisabeth cracks a rare smile. "Well done. You are the first one to answer that correctly. Well, after me that is," she says conspiratorially. "Follow me." We walk down the hall. We come upon a door that opens to Elisabeth's office. "I would like you to try something."

She pulls out a piece of wood with 16 circular indentations carved into the surface in the shape of a square, four by four. She pulls out thirty small balls—fifteen gray, fifteen white—the same size as the pits on the board.

"Ever since I was young, strategy games have been my favorite. I want to see what you make of this ancient game called Pylos. The rules are actually quite simple. We alternate turns to build a pyramid. If, in the process of placing your balls, you can successfully make a four-by-four grouping of your color on any single level of the pyramid, then you may remove either one or two of the balls that formed that square. The goal is to place the final piece on the top of the pyramid, understand?"

"Yes," I say as she passes me the gray pieces, keeping the white for herself.

"You can go first," she says staring at me.

I place a smooth ball on the board and await her turn. The first placements seem easy, and I begin to question the complexity of the game. But then I am faced with options that seem to have no satisfactory outcome—Elisabeth creates four by four squares and deftly removes balls from the board as I continue to expend mine. I am faced with trap after trap. She wins by a large margin.

"Good game. We will play again next week, and the week after that until you win or give up."

I won't give up.

•—•—•

"I didn't even think of that. I mean I didn't even know the lessons were a test until you figured it out, and I have never even heard of that game . . . ." Mallory trails off.

"You were the one to figure that out, not me," I say.

"She sees you as her equal." Mallory continues, not paying attention to what I had said.

"What? No, I wasn't even able to get close to beating her."

"That does not matter. She showed you the game because she thinks you're equal to her; she thinks you could beat her; she thinks that you are like her. She thinks you can be a leader."

•—•—•

The next week I finish my lessons and come back to the compound to find Mallory already slumped in a chair. She doesn't speak as I take a seat next to her. We both sit quietly in the lobby not talking like we normally do. She thinks she's done. None of the leaders have taken any particular of interest in her like they have in me. Charles had been involved in my training from the beginning and was likely the one who picked me for future leader. If Mallory is right, both Elisabeth and Jenna have taken an interest in me as my lessons have progressed. Unless the last leader is advocating for her to stay, well, unfortunately, she's as good as gone. They don't need her if they have me.

Chapter 16

PURPOSE

"Charles, shut up!"

"Jenna, I will not! I—"

Elisabeth walks into the room. "Not bickering again are we?" Neither speaks. "This isn't about Charles's library again, is it?" Immediately Charles and Jenna start talking. "I'm sorry I asked," and they both stop.

Jenna finally speaks. "Elisabeth, we are ready to start the final subconscious test whenever you are."

Elisabeth nods her head, and a screen begins to flicker, then glow, showing a gray rectangular room with a pane of glass separating a girl and a bleeding man. They watch, fixated on the screen as time and time again the girl tries to save the man, banging on the glass, trying to break through.

"Mallory knows that he committed a heinous crime and was sentenced to death by the Collective, right?" Elisabeth asks.

"Yes," Charles answers.

"How can somebody so smart be so foolish? Doesn't she know it is some people's purpose to die?" Jenna says. "At least we know she has no selfishness." The three laugh.

"No matter how many times we have tried, we can't break through that impenetrable wall of compassion and empathy," Charles says. "So brilliant. What a waste," he adds.

"Contact Oswald. We need to decide what to do with her," Elisabeth curtly says, "she may yet serve a purpose."

Chapter 17

FILES

Elisabeth has badly beaten me at her game. Again. I'm wallowing in my defeat on the ride back to my compartment in the pod when I notice Mallory is behaving strangely. She has been completely quiet. Normally, even when she has had a bad day, she says something about it. I ask her what's wrong and she furtively surveys our surroundings before saying in hushed tones, "I… I found something, but we can't talk here."

"Ok," I say tentatively. Something is definitely wrong. I can't tell what, but there's a coldness in her voice that hasn't been there before. I decide to push the matter further and ask, "where *can* we talk?"

"When we get off the pod, follow a little behind me, but make sure no one sees you," she whispers. I nod tentatively and sit quietly for the rest of the ride back to the compound, wondering what could be so important and so secretive.

Mallory steps out of the pod, then furtively looks around, waiting until the others leave before walking along the side of the building and disappearing around a corner. I follow just fast enough to see her slip behind a sprawling bush in a slightly overgrown area of the grounds where untrimmed grass and weeds protrude from the otherwise immaculate cement walkways. I am nearly to the bush when I stop, realizing how weird this is. I turn back, about to return to the main entrance, when a group of people walk around the corner. I duck into the bush and disappear into the foliage less than a second before they look up, scan the area, and continue to walk along the back of the building. They are wearing white, like everyone who lives in the compound, but there's an unseemly bulk to their posture—a bulk of concealed armor and weapons. They swagger in a pathetic attempt to mimic the authoritative ease of the leaders and other officials, and I easily identify them as guards.

I see Mallory crouched in the bushes. She places a finger to her lips, instructing me to be quiet. We wait as the guards round the corner and walk away.

I stand and she pulls me back into the grass.

"There's no one here. What's the big deal?"

"They are always watching," she whispers.

"I'm sorry, what?"

She doesn't reply. I sit in the bushes and wait. When she finally speaks, it is in a nearly unintelligible fast whisper. "So today I was supposed to have a meeting with Charles, but it got canceled, Oswald is coming back soon and they needed to make preparations. I had nothing else to do, so I went to his office to ask him if I could go to the library, but he never showed up. I took the opportunity to open the cabinets in his office."

"You-you did what?" I say in disbelief.

"I thought it might have information as to how I could be better. I think they're going to reassign me soon," she says looking down.

"But you would be the perfect leader."

"I don't think they agree. Anyway, the cabinet it—it's filled with files upon files of papers, like in the books, that detail something called 'raids.' That's why there is no account of the Outsiders perspective. We are killing them all. Or if not killing them, absorbing them into the Collective in the lowest positions. No one pays attention to them, and they are forced to work for the Collective." I suppose that could be true. No one would pay attention to former Outsiders. After Assignment, everyone is expected to fulfill their role, no matter what it is, and not question it.

"There's more. There were no peace talks between the Collective and the Outsiders. There was no effort to find a way to coexist. The Collective just decided they—we—were better and started killing anyone who disagreed," she says.

"Why would they lie?" I ask.

"To have control. That is what they want. That's their motive," she says. I remember her talking about motives, and how she thought that in order to fully understand someone, you need to know their motive. Without knowing the 'why,' you can never understand them, never beat them.

"Hold on. If what you're saying is true, what are you planning on doing exactly?"

"I don't know. Something . . . ." she says. She hesitates before meeting my eye, "There's one more thing, in one of the files," a pause. "Well, I . . . I don't know how to tell you this. You were born on the outside, and your mother was their leader. They found her and took her back here, someplace in the Collective, and they tortured her, trying to get any information, but she didn't tell them anything." She's starting to cry. "Elisabeth . . . she made her play the same game she's playing with you, only for her life. Your mom never lost until Elisabeth told her about you. Elisabeth told her that they had found you and that you were going to be a leader in the Collective and there was nothing she could do. That day she was executed—she had stayed alive for you. But then she gave up . . . ."

"What? Are you sure?" I ask.

"Positive. I'm sorry." She's crying harder now.

"You don't need to apologize. You didn't do anything." I take a deep breath, "They did."

"We need to talk about it. We need to do something," she implores. "We must talk more tomorrow. It's almost 9:30."

"We don't want to get stuck out here," I note with a bit of unease.

"Yes, just remember to cover your face when you go back in."

It's getting dark, and we both know that chips will be putting us to sleep soon. I pull my shirt over my head and run bowlegged back to the compound. Staying in the shadows as much as possible, I quickly walk up the stairs and make it up to my room. I need to think about what Mallory has just told me. My bed in the corner seems so close, and I almost make it, but my chip puts me to sleep barely seconds after I cross the threshold, and I fall face-first into the hard floor.

Chapter 18

GONE

I wake on the floor of my compartment. My knees and one side of my face are sore. I pull up the legs of my pants to expose two large purple bruises. I quickly stretch my back and hear it crack. I look at my reflection and realize that I am lucky enough to not have a bruise on my face. It's only a bit squished. I hurry over and wash my clothes in the shower to get the grass stains off. I rub them with soap for several minutes before the stains lift. I don't want to incriminate myself. I leave my soaked clothing hanging in the shower to dry. I dress in fresh clothing and try to get my hair, still short but now growing, to look presentable. I head for the pod, jogging down the stairs so I don't get left behind. Once I'm seated, I look around, trying to find Mallory, but I don't see her. Maybe she went in early. Given I have nothing better to do, I access my itinerary and look at the schedule. "'Meeting with Charles" is highlighted at the top of the list. This is out of the ordinary because for the past few days all I have been doing in the morning is playing that cursed game with Elisabeth, but I guess this will be a nice break. After all, I haven't seen Charles in a while.

•—•—•

I knock on the door and hear Charles telling me to enter. I walk in and see him facing the wall. I clear my throat and he turns. "Why don't you sit down." I hesitate, and he continues, "You were friends with Mallory?" I slowly nod my head in confirmation. Charles sighs, "last night a guard saw someone hiding on the outskirts of the compound. Suspecting an intruder, the guard followed the appropriate protocol and shot the suspicious person. Once they were positive the threat had been neutralized, the guards went to inspect the body. It wasn't an Outsider. It was Mallory. We don't know why, but she was in a bush, apparently stuck outside the building."

Charles' voice gets quieter and quieter as it is replaced with buzzing in my head that grows louder every second. She can't be. How was this allowed to happen? I put my head in my hands as the sound of her voice fills my ears. I hear nothing but her voice, see nothing but her face; all I can comprehend is our last whispered discussion. Reminding me to cover my face to keep me from being cut. Telling me to go first.

"She trusted you, I trusted you, how could you let this happen," I sputter.

"I didn't. It wasn't my fault, please calm down," Charles says.

"No, NO, I will not calm down," I shout at him. "You could have if you wanted to."

"I had no control over what happened."

I remember Mallory worrying that she was going to be reassigned. Had they done this on purpose? Were they really that selfish? "I want to be alone."

"Are you sure? I can stay if you want me to."

"I'm sure, get out." He doesn't leave so I scream, "get out, get out, out!"

Charles gets up and leaves. I grip my head tightly, pressing my hands against my ears to stop the noise. I close my eyes, trying to hold onto her. I picture her face. The last thing she had said keeps repeating in my brain, again and again. I look up and see the cabinet Mallory had mentioned. It's slightly off center, presumably from when she had opened it. Numbly, I get up and reach for the handle. The drawer opens easily. The papers are slightly askew. I pull out a file.

I pour over the pages, wanting to see if what she had said is true. She was absolutely right. The cabinet is full of pages upon pages of "raids." People having their freedom torn from them as they were forced to choose between death or the lowest jobs in the Collective.

I wipe my eyes to clear the tears, and that is when I see the interrogation of an Outside leader Mallory had spoken of. My mother. I push the flooding emotions away in an attempt to find something useful, something that could help me. There are detailed accounts of the games they played. I force myself to focus on the details, to glean some sense of motive. It's clear that Elisabeth uses the game to understand her opponents, how they think, their strategies, thoughts. She's doing the same to me, slowly chipping away at my freedom. It is then I decide. I will leave the Collective, for Mallory, who never got the chance to be free. For my mother, who had her freedom taken from her. And I will find out where I came from.

Chapter 19

STARS

I stare across the table, looking into Elisabeth's cold eyes. I've plastered a convincing enough smile across my face. After seeing all the matches that my mother and Elisabeth had played, I now understand her weakness and use it against her. She's ruthless, aggressive, and in her arrogance, she always plays for a short-term benefit. The worst thing any powerful person can do is believe they are invincible, for in that moment they are weakest. Patience. That's the key to her undoing. I see Elisabeth falling into the same trap my mother used to set for her as the game proceeds. I watch as the corner of her lips imperceptibly twitch as she realizes that I will win. We play out the game as she tries to maintain some dignity in her loss. As I place the last piece on top of the pyramid, for the first time, I look up at Elisabeth and innocently say, "good game."

"Good game," she says. "I have some work to do. Have a good day."

"Thank you, I will." It all feels so surreal. I stand and leave the room. I walk past the pod that I would normally board. I don't take much trouble trying to hide; there's no one there who would look for me anymore. I walk in the direction of the meeting hall, knowing that no one will be there now, planning to climb to the top and try to find the edge of the Collective. I make it to the meeting hall where I had been assigned future leader, where I had left my old life behind. I wish I could go back to before the Assignment, before my life had been turned upside down. How naive I once was to believe everything they told me—to believe I was finally growing up. Now, I know where I belong, and it's not here.

•—•—•

I scour the skyline looking for a way to the Outside, but all I see are buildings and more buildings. I look down and see members of the Collective obediently carrying out their jobs and duties like little ants working to appease the queen. Alex must have had an idea as to where he would go once he escaped. That's when I see it: a long line of people stretching as far as I can see. They must be coming from the Outside.

I run down the stairs, not wanting to lose them. I don't think; I don't feel. The all-encompassing need to leave is overwhelming. So I run and run until my legs feel like they're burning and I'm gasping for breath, and even then I don't stop. Air burns in my lungs, and my stomach tightens. I run harder, faster, until the buildings blur. I know I must be getting farther away from the leader's compound. The streets are dirty and trash lines the road; forgotten and derelict equipment lies alongside dilapidated buildings. The contrast to the leader's compound is disorienting.

Hunched figures of what used to be Outsiders walk in a straight, orderly line, appearing not to notice me as I sprint past. Their feet stumble over cracks in the ground. Their cheeks are hollow; their eyes hopeless. They are already starting to lose themselves. I see a boy watch me as I pass. He's young, two or three at most, with sharp angles of bones showing through his shirt. Someday I'll help them, but now I need to leave. I wipe the image from my mind as best I can. Others, presumably those who are part of the Collective, watch the line of Outsiders. They make crude remarks, not caring if they are heard. Gap toothed yellow smiles and dirty faces watch the procession with burning hate. These individuals have been so downtrodden by the Collective that they jump at the chance to hurt others. It's clear that these people know how needy these newcomers are; they just don't care enough to help. So much for being selfless.

I hear a different set of voices nearby. Not cruel laughter, but a pompous, snide drawl: it can only be Oswald, the fourth leader. My heart starts pounding as

I look for someplace to hide. I dive into a dilapidated building and wait for him to pass.

I feel something warm on my arm and I raise it closer to my face. In the dim light, I can see that there's a jagged piece of glass embedded in my skin. I shudder. It's hard to believe people live here. My hand shakes as I grab the shard of glass and slowly pull it out of my arm. More blood gushes out of the wound. Clearly the glass had been staunching the flow. I quickly drop the shard and tear off a piece of fabric from my shirt. I use it to gently dab along my arm to remove some of the blood, preparing myself for what I need to do next. I gently probe my cut with my fingers trying to find any glass that may remain. I push them deeper into the cut, wincing silently, but all I feel is the warmth of my own blood. I hurriedly tie another strip of fabric over the wound. I sit, concealed by the building, not daring to breathe as I hear Oswald's voice getting closer.

"We got the largest number of people to join the Collective in years!" says Oswald, a tall blond-haired man who I've only seen in pictures on screens.

"Yes sir," says a guard. Two guards walk on either side of Oswald, while the rest of the soldiers walk in rows of three, marching in unison. They are unfocused as they laugh to one another. If one of the Outsiders wanted to leave, it would be so easy, but they are so broken they don't even try.

"Can't you ever say anything other than 'yes sir'?" Oswald laughs. "I mean, we've been out there for ages, and all you can say is still just 'yes sir,'" he continues mockingly.

"Yes sir," says the guard.

The next words are unintelligible, but I can tell Oswald is not happy with the guard's response. Eventually the yelling fades into the distance. Peering out of my hiding place, I see the last guard disappear around the corner, and the others who were watching disappear like ghosts into the buildings. I slink out of my hiding place and run along the shadows, hyperconscious of the bright white of my clothing that signifies I don't belong. As I run, the buildings begin to look worse and worse until plants are springing up from the cracked concrete and walls lie in heaps of rubble at my feet. Night is falling, and I need to find a safe place to spend the night, for I have no clue what lies beyond in the darkness.

I find a small building that's teetering, just at the edge of falling. It has a gaping hole in the roof, and only three walls remain standing. Although not the accommodations I am accustomed to, it'll do. I find some vines that had been crawling up nearby buildings and bring them back to cover the missing wall, obscuring my hiding place from the outside world. I clear an area of rock and make myself as comfortable as possible. When I look up through the hole in the ceiling, I see pinpricks of light appear upon the jet-black sky, illuminating the darkness. I realize that these must be stars.

Chapter 20

THE FOREST

open my eyes and feel a warm breeze and a tickle on my face. I hurriedly sit up and slap my face as hard as I can, trying to get whatever it is off. A little bug falls onto the ground and scurries away. I quickly get up and start walking away, feeling slightly embarrassed. In less than an hour, the leaders will notice that I am not in my compartment and will send someone to find me. I speed up my pace, wanting to put as much distance as possible between me and the Collective. The buildings have all but disappeared, noticeable as only flattened rubble here and there. Eventually I find myself in a plain of dusty ground with a few sticks of grass growing here and there. Not a good hiding place.

After an hour or two of walking, I see a large group of trees in the distance. I can hide in there. I hurry towards the grove, and as I get closer, my breath catches in my throat as I am awed by the trees that tower hundreds of feet into the air. My feet trip over the roots and brambles as the forest tries swallow me in its depths. I continue walking deeper into the forest, aware of every sound, breathing in an unfamiliar but pleasant scent. Flies buzz around me, smelling the mixture of sweat and blood. One lands on the piece of cloth I had hastily tied around my arm yesterday. I need to wash it soon: the blood has hardened and is chafing around the skin surrounding the cut. The heat is becoming nearly unbearable, and I need to either find some water or someplace where I can wait out the hottest part of the day.

I look for a hole or cave where I can escape from the heat, but then something tells me that this is not a good idea. Instead, I survey the trees as I'm walking, looking for a way to climb one. I see two trees that are both close together and whose branches are lower down than those of the surrounding ones. I walk over, looking up into the spider-like branches. There's enough coverage that there will still be substantial shade, and the wind will be stronger up there. I decide that this is my best option and lean my back against one and push with my feet against the other. I push as hard as I can and slowly work my way up the trunk. The bark scrapes against my back as I inch up to where the branches start to spring out from the tree. My legs tremble from the effort of pushing against the tree so hard, and my back feels as though it has been scraped raw, but I'm so close to the branches. If I give up now, I'll fall forty-odd feet to the ground.

I continue to painstakingly make my way up the tree until I can reach up and grab one of the branches. I pull myself onto it and catch my breath, shaking out my numb legs. I'm beginning to regret my decision to go this way. It took such a long time to climb up, and I'm exhausted. The sun has already sunk low on the horizon, and I hadn't made any more progress away from the Collective. But now that I'm here, I might as well stay until morning. It will be dark by the time I climb all the way back down, and I'm too tired to attempt it now. I just need to make it as high up as I can, to obscure myself as much as possible. I look up to try to find a good place to spend the night. There's an area that seems like it'll do the trick. The interwoven branches have created a sturdy, flat surface that is obscured by the dark, needle-like foliage. With the light quickly fading, soon it will be impossible to see from the forest floor.

I swing myself up higher into the tree. Finally, I reach the flat spot and heave myself over the side, rolling into the arms of the tree. It is quickly apparent that the surface is not as flat as I had previously thought as a stick pokes me in the side, small branches haphazardly protrude up, and large lumps bulge from the branches. I pull my sweater off, laying it on the rough tree limbs. Some of the smaller sticks poke through and I break them off.

My stomach reels as I look down at the forest floor. As I watch, the animals I had scared away slowly return in the fading light. They're reclaiming what is theirs. Humans are but temporary inhabitants in nature, I think. We momentarily change things as we see fit, but it inevitably is returned to its rightful state. I make myself as comfortable as possible, but I wish I had brought one of the pillows from my compartment with me. Going to sleep here proves much more difficult than the instant reprieve I am accustomed to, and I now need to get some rest before the morning. Too tired to think, I can only stare at the branches above me until they blur together and I finally fall asleep.

•—•—•

A twig snaps with a sharp crack, and I open my eyes. I think I'm falling, and I hold my breath waiting for the impact, but there is none. I'm still cradled in the branches of the tree; I had just rolled over, and my head was dangling over a dark nothing. I listen for the quiet of the forest to calm me once more. Instead, I hear the sound of feet drumming on hard earth. I tentatively sit up and hear boots stomping between the trees. The Collective has begun to search for me. Each soldier holds a light that casts a wide beam over the ground. They are looking for footprints. I look down at the tree I had climbed and, even in the minimal light that reaches me, I can see where I had scraped off the bark. About halfway up the tree, I see a glow of white. A fragment of cloth sticks to the tree, next to the muted dull tones of the forest it gleams like a beacon. However, the soldiers are not looking in the trees. They seem to think I would stay on the forest floor, and they do not cast their eyes upwards. I watch as the horde passes. Behind them they leave a wake of destruction. Everything that had been alive and peaceful is now trampled. They think everything is theirs, that everything belongs to them. How selfish. I can't believe I was once proud to be a part of the Collective.

Chapter 21

BEE

In the morning, I find the destruction even worse than what I could see from my bed in the tree. Being closer to the ground in the daylight, I see everything in more detail. The ground crunches under my feet as I precariously walk through trampled plants. The once-beautiful forest feels like a wasteland. Once again, it's my fault. I am glad I didn't sleep closer to the ground or I would have had the same fate. Luckily, no one will notice my footprints among the hundreds already stamped in the soft ground, and the Collective is too arrogant to think I might have outsmarted them. I start walking on the path they have cleared. The trees slowly shrink and are replaced by fields of tall grass that are nearly taller than I am. The destruction ends here—those seeking me had decided to go up a nearby mountain instead of going through the grass. Taking the obvious choice if I want to avoid them, I begin wading through the field. In a short time the grass completely obscures my vision. I do my best to walk in a straight line, wanting to get as large of a head start as possible before they find out that climbing the mountain was futile and come back. I need to go to a place they won't be able to find.

I burst out of the grass to discover a field dotted with brightly colored flowers. The edge of the field abruptly ends, presumably a drop off of some sort. Out of the corner of my eye, I see a flash. I look over and see a trickling stream of water. Eagerly I rush over, careful not to crush anything beneath me, and drink as much as I can before leaning against a warm nearby rock. Hidden in the grass are succulent wild berries. I leisurely put a few in my mouth, enjoying the tangy flavor and letting myself relax for a short time. I see a black and yellow bug lazily float past me before it lands on my arm. Its fluffy little body is covered with pollen, and a little cloud puffs up when it lands. Without hesitation, it proceeds to sting me. I shriek, not expecting the assault. The bee falls to the ground, dead. I look around and realize more of the bugs are hovering around some sort of nest in a nearby bush. They must think I am threatening their home. I carefully pry a tiny stinger out of my skin. It's astounding that this small animal with such limited neurological abilities can be so selfless, something that I had tried, and failed to do for years. To be willing to give one's life to protect others is something I know no one in the Collective would do.

Chapter 22

FIRE

I remove the bandage on my arm and scrub my wound in the cold water. Once the water runs clear, I wring the once-dirty cloth out and loop it around my arm before heading towards the drop off. The flowers contrast against the bright blue sky. I reach the edge of the field and look down. There's a small rock slide that leads into a long slow hill that meets the edge of . . . something. It resembles the decaying outskirts of the Collective, but it has more variation. All the buildings are different heights and shapes. It must have been a city, though it is now misshapen and appears utterly inhospitable from afar. The tops of most of the buildings are missing their roofs. One of the structures is split down the middle and one of the halves leans precariously against a nearby building.

I slide down the side of the hill to what appears to have once been a road and walk on its uneven surface until I reach the outskirts of the city. Glass crunches under my feet, and a small animal darts into one of the buildings. I peer around the corner and am greeted by a sharp hiss. I don't wait to see what made the sound but quickly back away and make my way around another building to get into the city.

As I walk, I see things that were invisible from the hill. There are a multitude of animals roaming the derelict city. Their beady eyes watch me reproachfully as I pass. The air whistles through the buildings, creating a haunting melody. What I believe to be cars lie abandoned on the side of the road, many with large bushes or trees growing from the interiors. Signs from old buildings lie on the ground with faded letters, and one dangles from the side of a building. It says, "Joe's Pizza $5 a Slice," with an image of a smiling man spinning a disk on his finger. A layer of dust has settled over everything, softening the sound of my steps.

I hear a snap in the distance and duck behind a building. A large animal with antlers the size of tree limbs and a coat so sleek it looks as if it's glistening is standing in the middle of the road. It walks over to a car and begins to eat the grass growing out of the window. I lean forward to get a closer look. The animal flicks its large ear toward the horizon and freezes with its gaze fixed on the edge of the city. It hesitates a moment before strolling unconcerned down an alley and out of sight.

I then see what it had been looking at—a figure on the hill above the city. As more and more figures appear on the hill, I dart into a building and climb the semi-intact stairs until I burst open a door and find myself on the rooftop. There's a large chunk of some machinery lying on the roof. I struggle to lift it and wedge it against the door to keep it from opening. Leaning against a chunk of concrete, I catch my breath. I'm unaccustomed to this much physical exertion. When I was a child, I was required to exercise regularly, but as I grew older, it was less and less important. School, at that point, was all about the Test. Some would still make an effort to exercise, but the majority of us focused on studies. Now I wish I had kept my body in better physical condition.

I'm woken from my thoughts by the sound of voices. I quietly walk to the edge of the roof and look down to see hundreds of people flooding the city. I nearly gasp as I recognize one from the trial—an individual who had attacked me in the shower. Do all the cut end up soldiers? They are running inside buildings, and many are running up to the roofs. I hit the ground and pull a large piece of rusting metal over me. The smell of old metal pervades my nose and I start to cough. That's not good. I try to stop myself, but under the sheet of metal, all the air is contaminated with the tangy odor. I push the metal down again and gasp for air. I hear a rattling and assume a group has made its way to my roof. I duck under the metal once more and hold my breath. I wait, hoping the door will hold. The rattling stops and I hear feet thundering back down the stairs.

I lift my head out and see that the people are gathering in the center of the city. One of them starts lighting a building on fire, trying to either smoke me out or kill me; I get the feeling they don't really care which. They set fire to the buildings that were closest to the hill. They must have assumed that I didn't make it too far in. They retreat back to the hill as the fire spreads. The sun has started to set, but there is plenty of light from the advancing inferno that darkness gives me no cover. I need to get out; under the metal, the heat of the fire feels like it's cooking me alive. I jerk away from the now ineffective, burning hot cover. The smell of metal is replaced by smoke. I pull my shirt over my nose and mouth and squint, trying to see through the smog. I can see that the Collective has crudely erected tents on the hill and the majority of figures have gone inside. Only a few stay awake, sentinels of the night. The fire doesn't get very high on the metal and cement construct I'd inadvertently chosen, but the smoke up here is oppressive. I don't dare try to climb down while the city is so brightly lit, so I huddle on the windward side, trying to muffle my coughing.

Once the fires burn down, I walk down the stairs, wishing they didn't creak so much. I sneak out the doorway and slide along the side of the buildings, hiding in the shadows they cast. One day I won't have to hide. I make it out of the city and watch the fire eat the last of the structures. A strong breeze sends the flames licking up high into the sky, a last effort for it to stay alive before it is swallowed by the darkness.

Chapter 23

WALL

After escaping the burning city, I force myself to walk a little way further into the wildness before I collapse from exhaustion in a grove of trees. My eyes flick open as the sun starts to glimmer on the horizon. I painfully get up from my cramped position and stretch. The night had been cold, and the brush offered no protection from the biting wind. The cold isn't my most pressing issue, though. I'm so hungry that my stomach becomes my only thought. That is until I also realize that I am also thirsty—the heat had sucked all the moisture out of me.

I mindlessly clean myself as best I can. I'm not accustomed to being so filthy. In the Collective, everything was always clean to the point of obsession. Here the best I can do is try to brush off the dust and ash from yesterday and wipe my hands in the tiny residue of dew that had formed around me in the night, but still it's better than remaining in complete filth. I squint my eyes to survey the skyline, looking for something. The Collective is sure to be watching the city, so returning there is not an option. In the distance, there's an outline of a mountain range. It's far, but I don't have another option, and I have at least an hour or two before they discover that I am not in the rubble of the city and move on. I also might find some water, or some berries. Anything.

•—•—•

I'm being hunted. I can feel it. I jog into an open plain towards the mountain range that stretches off to both the right and the left, blocking my path. I don't like the idea of going high up—it seems the higher I am, the easier time they have finding me, but it's the only option. I look back and see the city getting smaller and smaller, now barely a smudge at the base of a lumpy green hill. Hopefully, they'll search the other direction before coming this way.

Every breath feels like a chore, dragging the hot, thick, still-smoky air in my parched throat and pushing it back out. I'm almost to the foot of mountains when I see someone running onto the open plain. I can't tell whether or not they see me, but I sprint the remainder of the way to the mountains. I duck behind a rock and look up, noticing for the first time how bad of a choice it was to come here. Towering above me is a tall granite wall. I can't go back and risk exposing myself; I am going to have to climb up. I tie my sweater around my waist and roll up my pants. I look absurd.

I reach up and take hold of a divot in the wall, then pull myself up. Slowly I start to climb the wall. When I'm roughly halfway up, I look back and see more figures moving across the plain, spurring me upward. Breathing is difficult. Every second I try to cling to the sheer wall is agony, but somehow I climb faster. The sharp hot stone pulls and tugs at my skin, ripping it. I reach up and grab hold of the rock above me. It gives way, and I'm left dangling in midair only holding on with one hand. A fierce wind pushes me against the rock and my arms burn as I try to pull myself up. I grunt and pull myself to another hand hold. My feet scramble against the wall trying to find footing on the smooth rock. I let out a scream of frustration. My feet finally find a perch, and I keep climbing, this time ensuring each handhold will hold my weight first. When the soldiers do arrive, I'm hoping they'll think I couldn't have gone this way, or that I went around the hill. Only a very foolish person would try to climb as I am now.

My hand reaches up to find nothing, and I realize I've finally reached the top. The last push is agonizing, but my free arm finds a root or a bush or something, and I'm able to drag my body up the last few feet. I roll onto the top of the wall and look over the edge to see the first few figures arriving at the bottom of the wall. I bring my hands to eye level and notice that they are bright red; a layer of skin has rubbed off, leaving my fingers and palms oozing and tender. I can't rest for too long in case the soldiers decide to climb the wall. I get to my feet and begin jogging across the plateau, allowing my arms to dangle limply at my sides. I reach the other side of the ridge to discover, fortunately, that there is not another cliff, but instead a slow decline onto another plain. There is no water, no food, and no place to hide up here. My only option is to head directly onto the plain and hope the others don't make it over anytime soon.

Chapter 24

SPAGHETTIOS

The light filters through the window frame. Dust particles swirl in the morning light. My legs ache as I get up. I had found this place in the middle of the night and did not have the opportunity to inspect my new surroundings. Now, however, I can clearly see the structures that tower into the sky. This was once a lively place; colorful peeling paint is partly visible on the buildings; enthusiastic signs lie forgotten on the ground or barely hang on to the buildings. I carefully step over the piles of broken glass. The tinkling of the glass shifting reverberates in the concrete oasis. All around me there are illustrations that must have once been inviting but are now faded and sinister. On nearly every surface there are rows of blown out light bulbs, an obsolete technology that has been long replaced. A grinding of metal makes me jump. I spin around, heart racing. But there's only a sign swinging eerily in the breeze.

Inside the buildings, there are hundreds of machines which have been well-protected by the buildings. They look new. I walk down row after row of these machines, wondering their purpose. The faded red carpet muffles my footsteps, making me feel as if time itself is slowing. I notice a little door on the side of one machine; it's locked, but there's a gap between the door and its frame. I find a metal bar and wedge it into a crack, then push down. The lock breaks, and the little door swings open. Small slips of green paper fly out. They cover the floor, and I pick one up to examine it. There's a little face on one side, I flip it over, the other has a tiny building. I rip it in half. Nothing. What is this and why is there so much? Then it dawns on me. I had read that this is how people used to distinguish worth. The more you had, the more important you were, and yet so many gambled it away. Money, such a useless thing. An object that promotes a feeling of superiority, of power. People have killed over this. Useless bits of paper. Now look, a fortune here for anyone who wants it, but no one wants it. I kick the pile with my foot, sending it flying across the floor. Disgusting. I try to find a way out of the sprawling labyrinth I now know was used as a trap. The bright colors and inviting designs drew people here and kept them here until they lost all of their "worth."

I finally find an exit, but as I'm leaving, I see a building with crisp white walls that remind me of the Collective. I walk inside and see stockpiled bandages, ointments and other medical equipment tucked neatly into sealed cabinets. This was once a hospital, I realize. I pull out some fresh bandages and wrap them around my hands and arm, then I search for a storage room and try to find some food. I haven't eaten in a long time, and my stomach now feels like it is eating itself. I stumble upon what must be a cafeteria, and excitedly pull open each cabinet. Most are empty. I keep looking until I find a full cabinet of "sardines," whatever that is. I grab a can and follow the directions to open it. A horrendous smell bombards my nose and I gag. There are little animals staring at me with dark, blank eyes. I shudder and place the lid back over their tiny coffin.

Growing more desperate, I continue to search drawers, cabinets, and closets for anything I can eat. Just when sardines seem like a reasonable option, I find a can of "SpaghettiOs." I pry the lid open with the butt of a knife, hoping there are no more dead animals inside. Instead I see a red soup with a little yellow rings floating in the mixture. I fold the metal lid into a spoon and taste it. It's not bad. It would be better warm, but there is no way I am going to take the time to heat it. I take the can with me as I find my way out of the hospital. Once outside, I sit on a chunk of upturned concrete and finish my "SpaghettiOs." What a stupid name.

Chapter 25

RAIN

Rain turns the dirt into mud, and it suctions my shoes, trying to pull them off with each step. Shivers go up my spine as the cold seeps deep into my bones. At least I'm not dehydrated anymore. I pull my soaked sweater tighter around my shoulders in a vain effort to stop them from shaking. The rain is starting to fall harder now, and I squint my eyes, trying to see, but it's becoming impossible. I can barely see my own hand. I look back expecting to see my footprints behind me, but instead the ground has been wiped clean. I suppose that may be good. I shift my gaze back to the rain and try to see if there is anything worth moving toward when my foot catches on something deep in the mud. My other leg slides on the slick ground and my foot comes free as I slip, landing face first in the wet earth. I groan and sit up, wiping my face. I try to stand, but I feel my feet slip under me again, and I fall back into the mud. I scramble to my feet, regaining my balance. I raise my face to the sky, letting the rain pour over my face, washing the dirt and mud away in a freezing shower. I can't do this anymore. I push the water out of my hair and look at the ground only to see the same brown sludge that is all around me. What am I doing here? Why am I even trying to run? I should just give up, just lie down and die here, in the middle of nowhere. My tears become unnoticeable in the downpour.

Chapter 26

FREEDOM

A large building looms in front of me as the sun slowly peeks over the horizon. I stumble closer, dragging my feet with each step. The rain stopped falling about an hour before dawn only to be replaced by a frigid breeze. I force my eyes open and see something strangely familiar. Tall buildings with blown out glass and faded signs. I can't quite put my finger on it until its dawns on me. My sluggish brain slowly comprehends that this is the same city I had left in the morning.

•—•—•

The sun is disappearing behind buildings when I finally open my eyes again. No, no, no, I get up and brush myself off. I had draped my sweater over a rock before falling into an exhausted sleep, and it is finally dry. Now

I grab it and try to pull it on as I start walking. It gets stuck on my head, and I teeter to the side trying to free myself, but I slam into a wall. I need to get away from this cursed place.

I must keep going. After realizing that I had gotten turned around in the rain, I had been too tired to keep going. I laid down to rest, promising myself that I would only stay a couple hours. That had not worked out well. As the sun drops below the horizon, I start to jog into the plain that has already sucked up the entirety of last night's rainstorm, but the pain in my stomach forces me to turn around and draws me back to the hospital. I am now desperate, I think, as I stare at the little fish in their dead eyes. The gnawing in my stomach wins out and I put one in my mouth. I try not to think, just swallow. My body rejects the slimy thing initially and I gag as it gets stuck in my throat. I force myself to swallow, and the sardine slowly slides down my throat. I shudder before moving on to the next.

•—•—•

A day passes. I squint into the distance, at first thinking I'm imagining things, but no, there, rolling green hills slowly come into view, illuminated by the sun that has been inching its way into the sky for about an hour. I had been starting to think that there was nothing out here, that I would never find anyone and would spend the remainder of my life running, and then die alone in a world I don't know. At least I got the chance to be in this world. This is a strange, but amazing place, filled with dangers, but most of all. . . I pause trying to think of the right word.

Freedom. It is freedom. Freedom to do what I want, when I want, and how I want to do it. Freedom to think whatever thoughts cross my mind without being pressured to force them back down again and again like I had for so many years, and how so many in the Collective are still doing. Or did. I know Mallory would have loved it here. The scent of grass floating on the breeze, the sound of the wind when it blows through the trees, and the way the sun goes down at night, painting the sky, then giving way to the stars. Oh, the stars, filling the sky with pinpricks of light, each bringing with it infinite worlds each with infinite possibilities.

One day I'll live amongst the stars and this will all be just an insignificant pinprick in the sky. The wind pushes back the little hair I've grown since the Assignment. I haven't given my hair a second thought in days; I simply don't need to anymore. Now that I have left the Collective, there is no need to conform anymore, no need to fulfill their expectations. I don't need to present myself as they want anymore. I finally understand how deeply I cared about what they all thought of me and how I wanted them to think of me. How they had changed me. How much I wanted to lose myself. For years I had tried not to draw unnecessary attention, to just become a part of the Collective. Not anymore. Now, I can grow my hair or I can keep it short. I can do whatever I want.

Chapter 27

HILLS

The next morning I wake to the delicious scent of fresh grass. I had fallen asleep at the base of one of the grassy hills, sheltered from the wind by a single large boulder. The light sparkles throughout the dewdrops on the green grass. I get up and immediately realize I need to look for something to eat. After a while of walking and seeing nothing, I climb a hill and look around, trying to find what direction I should go, but there are only the sprawling hills. I look back in the direction I had come and see how little progress I have made. In annoyance I sit down on the top of the hill. Something next to my hand suddenly moves and gives me a start. Before I know it, I'm rolling down the hill. At first, I am panicked, not knowing what's about to happen. Then I gently roll to a halt at the base of the hill and burst out laughing. I laugh so hard my stomach hurts and I need to catch my breath. I stand and run back up the hill and roll down again. This time, I try to gain momentum by starting at the highest point of the hill and letting gravity roll me down. My extra momentum sends me part way up the adjacent hill. I start laughing again as I lie in the warm grass. This is the most fun I've had in—I don't know how long. Fun—the thing which children find with ease but the older you become the more elusive it is. I haven't let myself be a kid—running in the sun, laughing until my cheeks hurt. For so long I had one focus: get a good grade on the Test so I would get a good Assignment. I thought that might be the end of it, but it's just gotten more severe. Pass the leaders' vetting and become a leader, trick them long enough to get out of the Collective, run, don't stop running until you find something. Don't sleep, don't rest, don't think of anything else.

I lie in the middle of the two hills with my eyes closed, just resting in the warm sun until I reluctantly stand and start walking again. Instead of walking tiredly between the hills, I now climb to the top of one and then roll down the other side. The ease of rolling down the hill makes up for the slightly fatiguing climb. I continue to do this until one of my rolls is cut short by an abrupt jolt to my shoulder. I look up to see what I had hit. It looks like a car with peeling red paint and rusty metal. I get up and brush myself off. Inside the car, the floor is covered with the soft grass and what looks to be a small tree, trying to force its way through the roof of the car. I carefully press on the metal and it crumbles in my hand. I create an opening by chipping out a jagged opening in the rusty metal. Almost gratefully, the tree springs out from its contorted shape. Inside the car, the leather seats are split, leaving stuffing and springs exposed. The tires sit near the car but are no longer attached. The pieces that once connected them to the car have long since rusted away, but the rubber of the tires remains intact. One of these is what my shoulder hit. I don't think I will be rolling down any more hills without checking the bottom first, I think sourly while rubbing my sore shoulder. I walk to the back of the car and see the large open compartment of sorts covered in grass and flowers. The walls of the car must protect these plants from the wind, allowing them to grow tall without being knocked down. That must be why these hills are so smooth. Whenever anything tries to grow, it must be beaten down by a fierce wind. Time and time again things must have tried to grow and been pushed down, but here, in what is just a pile of wreckage, something old and useless, life flourishes.

•—•—•

As day slowly turns to night, the light fades, sending colors chasing each other across the sky, turning clouds pink and sending golden light streaming down to earth only to be swallowed by the increasing darkness of night. Even then, however, light breaks through the darkness, illuminating the ground with a glow. The moon is high in the sky and sends light shining down as I lie on a flat top of one of the hills. I let the warm breeze brush my skin, occasionally sending my hair into my eyes. But I just leave it, letting it do what it pleases, because for the first time since I left the Collective a sense of calm dances in my brain, like a flower finally growing once it is shielded from the wind.

Chapter 28

WATER

It's nearing midday, and I need to look for water. I had pocketed some of the little fish from the hospital in the city, but those are about to run out. And they make me thirsty. I squint into the sky and see the expanse of blue unencumbered by even a hint of a rain cloud. It seems my only option is to try to find water on the ground. I walk between the hills, thinking some water may have collected there, but no luck. It seems that the hills have soaked up every ounce of water from the rain storm a few days prior. I search for what seems like hours—each minute I'm not moving away feels wasted—when I finally hear what must be a stream.

The hills cause the sound of the water to reverberate strangely so it's nearly impossible to find the true location of the source. When I finally find it, it is more of a trickle than a stream. The water is slowly oozing out of the side on the hill then dripping into a bright green pond. As I get closer, I see that the green is not from the reflection of the grass but a layer of thick algae that floats on the surface. I pluck a piece of grass and prod the algae with it. With a loud squelching noise the grass gets swallowed by the green ooze. Bubbles slowly rise to the surface and hover hungrily before swelling with gas, popping, and releasing a noxious fume into the air. Not wanting to provoke it, I slowly back away, not turning away from it until I am a safe distance. I don't want to risk being swallowed like that piece of grass. Odd, I think, how something that seemed so initially inviting could be so sinister.

Chapter 29

TREE

The sun shines into my eyes, blinding me. It wavers as the ripples on the water's surface disrupt its pristine reflection. Late last night I found this barrel of relatively clear water and drank as much as I could before passing out, leaning against its side. Now that the sun has risen, I should drink a little more, as I don't know when I might get another chance. Not far off, I can see a densely wooded area stretching across the horizon that will be difficult to get through. I grip the edge of the barrel to pull myself to my feet.

My legs feel like rubber. The constant movement and injuries I have endured have taken their toll. It feels so safe here and all I want to do is sleep, just for a few more hours.

I drink out of the barrel before making my way to the edge of the forest. I pull a few vines out of the way as I stumble through the dense undergrowth. It pulls at my legs, trapping them in the tangle of roots, fallen branches, and thorns. Birds screech in indignation as I blunder through their forest. With each step, I stop to disentangle myself. Even though I'm still putting in as much effort as possible, my body is slowing down; it can't go on for much longer.

I feel a droplet of sweat trickle down my neck, and my breathing is now ragged. I need to stop to rest. I weave my way deeper through the forest until I find a tall gnarly tree. The tree has many low hanging branches and protruding limbs: it will be easy to climb. Higher up in the tree there is a canopy of branches which seem to be large and sturdy enough to support my weight. I start the climb into the branches. When I reach the canopy, I'm disappointed that it seems even less smooth than the tall tree where I had spent the night at the beginning of my journey, but my tired body doesn't seem to mind the branches and knobs so much anymore. I stretch out on the long limb, finding a soft piece of moss to lay my head on, and fall into a light sleep.

Chapter 30

RIVER

I wake to the sound of shouting in the distance. I'm instantly alert, and the pain in my limbs is all but forgotten as the instinct to flee takes over. I roll out of the tree and fall to the ground, a jarring distance, but I hadn't been willing to push my body to climb very high. I take a deep breath and begin to run as fast as I can away from the voices. Branches whip against my face. A trickle of blood runs down my cheek. The voices get louder.

"This way. Through those trees, there!"

The pounding of feet grows louder. I run faster through the trees, but not fast enough. My heart is pounding out of my chest as I think I hear them getting close. Twigs snap, leaves crunch. Everything that I would have paid no attention to before is now all consuming. Any clue that I can glean from my surroundings as to where they are could be useful. I need to find some way to escape. Maybe it is possible to run around my pursuers and move in the opposite direction. But if everyone who helped burn the first city has come here, the line of soldiers might stretch out for miles. I discount it as an option and turn my full attention to keeping ahead of them. Every sound, even the ones I make, terrifies me as I become more irrational, more panicked. I need a plan, something I can follow if I lose control. Climbing a tree could work, but if I were located, I would have no way to escape. I'm running out of feasible ideas when I hear rushing water in the distance. If I can get across the water, it might slow them enough that I'll have time to hide. The river could also hide my tracks. It's by no means the best idea, but it's the only one I have left.

The sound of the water grows deafening as I get closer. The trees and brush fall away suddenly and I get my first view of a vast highway of rushing water. I skid to a stop. The ground is slick, and I grab onto a tree branch to keep myself from sliding into the water. I watch the rushing rapids beneath my feet. If this is going to work, I need to hurry. I try to slide down the hill holding the branch. I am halfway down, but the branch is at the end of its length. I hear a loud snap and fall into mud, trying to find something to grab onto. The mud provides no grip. There is a tuft of grass barely holding on to the dirt. I grab it, hoping it might hold my weight, but in reality I know even before taking hold that it will simply tear from the soil. I slide further. Water splashes at my feet, threatening to pull me under. I desperately try to keep myself from sliding into the water when I see it: a rock out in the middle of the river. It is far, but maybe, just maybe.

I can hear voices shouting over the sound of the rushing water. It's my only choice. I use my last seconds on land to try to jump to the rock. I don't jump far enough. The water pulls me under. I try to get my bearings, but I'm being tossed in every direction. I struggle towards the surface, but find myself being buffeted against the bottom of the river. I try to resist gasping, but my lungs are beginning to burn. I try to use the river bottom to push towards the surface. The cold air whips across my face, and I have just enough time to gasp before I am pulled back under. I am spun around and around in the raging water. A rock looms out of the darkness. I reach out, attempting to grab it. I miss. A current twists my arm away a second before the back of my head slams against the rock. I continue to swirl around in the water, unconscious.

Chapter 31

LOST

"Where, where, where!" screams Elisabeth.

"I, I don't know, please try to calm yourself," pleads Oswald.

"No, NO, I will not," she shouts. "All this work, all this time we have put in and, and. . . ." She sits in her chair, head in her hands.

"I don't understand! How did it turn off?" Charles starts saying but is promptly interrupted by Jenna.

"Chips only turn off if the user is dead or it becomes detached from the nervous system."

"I thought that only we could detach it, and doesn't that take a long time?" asks Charles.

"If something hit the chip hard enough, and in the correct spot, it could cause it to malfunction, and we have no data on that," she finishes quietly.

"And why do we have no data on that?" Elisabeth demands, "Why didn't you test it on the cuts?"

Charles and Jenna look at each other accusingly, "That, I believe, is my fault," a voice pipes up. "I believed it prudent to recruit those who got cut to join me in the looking for the Outsiders. Also, this kind of testing would have resulted in many casualties, would it not?" Oswald adds, looking imploringly at Jenna.

"Yes." she says. "And- and at least Charles had the idea to update the chip to have a tracker after the incident in the showers."

"A shocking instance of genius. Well, if you all don't find a way to track that chip, we will have three subjects for testing the theory, won't we." Elisabeth says quietly. The others nod. Her message is clear. They file out of her office.

"Who has any ideas?" Oswald starts saying before Jenna and Charles simultaneously shush him. Confused, Oswald silently follows them around the corner and out of earshot. Jenna whispers "I can try to send some sort of update. If part of the chip is still functional, it might respond, but it needs to be in range of another chip. The update normally bounces from chip to chip; that's how it travels so well in the Collective."

"Well, what if we send out soldiers to try to get in range? Then it would be able to update. Right?"

"Maybe, but it would be very difficult to ensure that they would be close enough," notes Jenna, always the contrarian. "And it will only work if there is a clear line of transmission—we can only detect it if the chip is high enough."

"Well, what other option do we have?" Charles asks.

They look at each other. No one says a thing. There is no other option.

"We better hope this works," Charles says resolutely. They solemnly nod to one another, then part ways.

Chapter 32

THE OUTSIDERS

I blearily open my eyes and see lights swimming above me. I try to sit up, but my head is dizzy, so I immediately lie back down. From the other side of the room I hear someone say, "look." There's a murmur of anticipation, and a crowd forms around the table I'm lying on.

I instantly know that these people are not from the Collective. They are shabbily dressed, and their clothing is adorned with multi-colored patches from being haphazardly mended over many years. There are stains and tears, and the clothing is generally ill-fitting. The faces above these motley items don't look right either. Lines from constant years of worrying are etched into their skin, marring their young faces. Their cheeks are hollow, and they have heavy shadows under their eyes. Yet, I catch a glimpse of a sparkle in nearly every eye I meet.

"Who are ya?" A woman's voice pops up from behind my head.

I crane my neck but can't figure out who's spoken. Reproachfully I reply, "who are you?"

"Chris. I'm the leader of the," she pauses, "well yu'd know us as th' Outsiders." The speaker moves into view. She seems very familiar. She looks about 27 and has shoulder-length dark brown hair and an old scar that runs the length of the left side of her face. She continues, "And yu're?"

I don't say anything. Chris's accent is different from that of the Collective, though not difficult to understand. The group waits expectantly. People shuffle in the small space, many pairs of eyes boring into me like I'm a specimen on a display table.

"You already know, don't you," I say after a moment.

Chris smiles. "Ya, we do. Ya jacket had ya name on it. we jus' wanted to see if yu'd tell us."

A man's voice cuts in saying, "we otta-," but he is interrupted by Chris.

"Can y'all leave? I need to talk with our, uh, guest."

The congregation obediently shuffles out, leaving Chris and me alone in the room. She waits for a moment, then goes over to the door and bangs the wall, shouting, "I said scram, Will."

"Fine I'm goin'," I hear a huff and the sound of feet shuffling away.

"OK, now they're gone." She hesitates before quickly saying, "do ya know anyone named Alex? He's my little brother. Anyways, we gottum in there when he was really little to learn about the Collective and leave after he was assigned to a low level job. They ain't pay no attention to those, but he was suposta be here by a while ago, and, well, he's not." I feel all the blood draining from my face. That is why she seemed so familiar, and that is why he tried to run. He knew death was better than being cut, forced to become a soldier and hunt down his family. "Do ya? He'd be about ya age," Chris says anxiously.

"Yes. He, uh," I'm not sure how to put it, "he was killed during the Assignment. He was cut, and he tried to run."

She sits back in her chair. A flood of emotions momentarily pours across her face before she has the forethought to conceal them. It seems as though she's been expecting to hear this sooner or later. I don't know how to comfort her, so I say the first thing that comes to mind. "He was my best friend, and I don't know if you got to see him much, but he was funny and kind and, and he always put others above himself, no matter the cost." I stop, unable to say anything further without the guilt being palpable in my voice.

Chris smiles sadly, "Then he took after our father. Papa didn't want 'em to go, but I insisted. We knew nothing about them or their strategies or plans or how their technology worked. I promised he'd be safe. Alex said he'd never forget us and would do his best to make us proud." A tear glistens in Chris's eye. She looks like she'll hold it in, but then her face contorts, and she gets up abruptly, wiping at her face, and leaves.

Chapter 33

OCEAN

I sit alone in the hut for hours waiting for something to happen. My dizziness is gone, but I don't know if I am allowed out or if I am supposed to stay here and wait for someone to fetch me. The musty smell of water and dust mix in the air to make an unsettling odor. In the Collective, everything always smelled clean and slightly antiseptic. I had never thought about it before, but here, where everything is different, I realize what it was really like in the Collective. I brush my hand against the worn, soft fabric of the clothing I had found myself in when I had woken up. I pull my jacket tighter around me.

I wait a few more minutes, and when nothing happens, I get up and walk around the small room examining it. Small glass bottles line the dusty shelves and bandages are messily piled in a basket in the corner. The light above me is a candle that sends shadows dancing up the walls. The flickering light adds to the air of unclean-liness I associate with those assigned to the lowest jobs in the Collective. A thin trail of stitches on my upper arm casts an unexpected lumpy shadow. I raise my hand to feel the puckered skin. My body is now riddled with cuts and bruises. I feel along these minor abrasions until my fingers find their way to my back. It's been covered in a thick layer of bandages and ointments, and I wince as I feel the rasp of broken skin when I stretch my arm around my ribs. I decide against probing the bandaging farther. Instead, I look out the small weathered window to see the blurry outlines of several figures in a mottled landscape of dusty green and tan under a bright blue sky. I open the creaky door of the shed, and a burst of cold air blasts my face and sends a shiver down my spine. I wrap my borrowed jacket tighter around my shoulders as I walk towards the others.

The medical shack sits atop one of the many small hills in the area. Clumps covered in sand and tall patches of grass spread out before me in gentle sloping hills. Beyond them, there is a steep incline with a large forest sitting atop. On the other side, the sand hills gently slope down to . . . What is that? I take a few steps forward and take in more of what I can only describe as an extraordinarily large pond. As I walk, the small hills grow progressively smaller until I reach the edge of the water. It rushes up the sand to greet me. The brilliant blue of the sky contrasted with the deep, almost ominous color of the water is overwhelming. I squint, looking for edges encircling this water. I do not see any. All I can see is the infinite blue. Then it hits me—this is an ocean. The enormity of the realization is dumbfounding. I can hardly imagine the never-ending sky and the wonders beneath the ocean's surface. I look along the shore—how strange it doesn't go farther—that it stops and gives way to an endless expanse. I sit on the sand and watch the waves slowly retreat and then be pushed forward by another wave. A sense of peace enters my brain and my muscles relax. I stare at the place water meets the sky, expecting to see land where there is none. The sun's reflection off the water is nearly as bright as the sun itself.

I made it. I escaped the Collective and found a place to survive. I won't be alone for the rest of my life.

I do not know how long I sit watching the water as waves appear in the distance and slowly travel towards me until finally reaching the land. After what might be moments or days, I hear a voice calling me back to reality. I stand and walk into the center of the village. There, someone hands me a bowl filled with something weird and gloopy. I look around and see others scooping it into their mouths with wooden spoons, so I follow suit. I stand awkwardly, not knowing where to go. In the Collective, only those in the leader's compound ate together, and even then, it was more of an obligation to be taken care of while those still downstairs completed their work. Here, people chatter and share some sort of flat grain-based discs. The meal seems more like a social event than a utilitarian exercise, so I try to slow my eating. It's difficult to swallow the strange goo anyway.

"Come'er," says the friendly voice of a man who has noticed my predicament. I head over and sit quietly as the others talk. Some furtively glance in my direction.

"So, what's yer story?" the man next to me says, nudging me in the side.

"Uhh," I'm hesitant to share much. I suspect that if I tell them about my Assignment, it won't go over well. I think quickly. "Well, I grew up in the Collective, but I left after they killed my friend. I quickly made the decision to tell them what I had learned before leaving the Collective. "Before I left, I was able to break into a leader's files and read about my life. It turns out that I was taken from the Outside when I was very young, apparently my mother was captured and interrogated because she was some sort of leader."

"Wait, hold on, are ya Haley's kid?" a voice asks.

"I don't know. The files never stated a name."

Everyone gets quiet. Then the whispers start.

"You know what, I kinda see it."

"No way, look at the nose, totally different."

Those assembled proceed to pick apart every piece of my appearance. I feel my face turning red, so I look at my feet. I've never felt this embarrassed about the way I look. In the Collective, everyone consciously avoided paying attention to how they or any one else looked, but things are different here. The man who had originally asked me the question clears her throat, silencing the whispers, and says, "Well then, welcome back."

Chapter 34

FISHING

I sit staring at the water. The ocean still amazes me. Chris sees me and asks, "Do ya wanna go on the water?"

"Yes," I say. I had seen large round wooden containers near the beach and assumed they were meant to float, but no one had taken one out yet. The prospect of getting to float on the glassy surface is intriguing.

"Yo, Will," Chris calls. When he doesn't respond, she hollers his name again, snapping for him to come closer. "Will, get a boat. The others and I are going huntin'." I look at Will's sour expression and my interest in boating dwindles significantly. I turn to tell Chris that I've changed my mind, but she is already out of earshot. Will and I look at each other. He rolls his eyes and walks to the boats with an audible huff. He is clearly no happier about this than I am. He angrily tugs at the old rope. His fingers slip on the slime for a few seconds before he eventually unties the knot freeing the boat. He starts pulling the rickety old thing towards the water before pausing, looking up, and saying, "ya gonna help?" I rush over. No matter how much I dislike him, I am still eager to go out on the water. He pushes me out of the way before pulling the boat the last few inches into the ocean. The boat bobs gently in the shallow water, and I admire it from the shore as I brush off my hands on my itchy pants.

"Grab the baskets and fishing poles." He jerks his hand towards a cluster of baskets and rods high on the beach, then continues under his breath, "maybe yu'll be useful for somethin'."

I ignore this, grab the things he gestured at, and climb into the boat. He pushes off from the shore, and I gingerly sit on the rickety seat. The boat seems to be slowly rotting away, but I know better than to say anything about it to Will. I sit in silence, watching the water rippling in the wake of the boat. I look up to see Will studying me. When his gaze meets mine, he looks away. I turn and watch as the small camp recedes until all I can see is water for miles around.

The sheer vastness of the ocean is shocking. Out of the corner of my eye, I see Will trying to pass me a fishing pole. I grab the smooth wood in my hand and mimic Will's motions as he deftly flings the line over the waves. I have little success. My line doesn't not reach as far as Will's, and I see him trying to hide a smirk. I sit and wait for something to happen. Nothing does. Will, however, seems to have great luck. I watch as one fish after another flops into his basket while I wait, feeling damp and useless. Suddenly I feel a yank on my line and start to reel it in as fast as I can. I raise my catch into the air. A tiny wriggling fish hangs on the end of my line. It is no larger than my thumb.

Will snorts, "Ya really are useless. That little thing isn't even good for bait. Throw it back and try again."

I do, and have just as much luck. We fish for hours, and I only manage to catch three fish that are to Will's liking. The sun is getting lower in the sky, sending a cascade of colors across the horizon and lighting up the glassy surface of the water with bright colors. I watch the reflection of the sky as it grows darker and darker.

I look up and see that Will is staring at me again. This time instead of looking away he quietly says, "why'd ya lie?"

"What do you mean," I ask.

"Do you know what I do?"

"No, how could I?" I say with a forced laugh.

"Do ya know how much I do for 'em? Do ya know how unnoticed all my hard work goes? I do the dirty work so no one else has to. Cleanin' all the clothing, storin' the food, watchin' the children when their parents ignore them. And I'm fine if they don't know, if they never notice, if they never listen to me if—if they don't care about me. I work so hard to keep 'em all safe, and I am not goin' to let ya mess that up. Do you wanna know what I found when I was washing the clothing? Well, I will enlighten ya if ya don't know. Every piece of your clothing was bright white. White is for leaders, but yu're too young to be a leader, so that means yu're a Future Leader. I knew at dinner when ya said ya were Haley's kid. There's no way ya wouldn't be one. And as always, I was the only one to see it. So, why did ya lie?" he says quickly.

"I-I didn't think it prudent to tell everyone that I was a Future Leader, but I-."

Will interrupts me saying, "Was?" He scoffs, standing in the boat, maintaining perfect balance even though a breeze blows over the water. "Yu're a Future Leader, and yu'll always be."

"No, listen to me," I begin to say. "That's not me! Not anymore . . . ."

He starts moving forward, and I stumble back and the little boat tips ominously low in the water.

"I've changed, really, I- I left them, I want nothing to do with them anymore!"

He lets out a sharp, cold laugh that chills my bones. "I don't believe ya. Yu'll always be part of the Collective."

"No, NO! I've changed. I really have," I shout. He quickly moves forward and before I know it, he has lifted me up as if I weigh no more than a child. I kick and scream, but there's no one to hear. I dangle over the dark water, bracing myself for the inevitable.

With tears in his eyes, Will says, "This is for the others, I need to protect them." Then he lets go.

The cold freezes my breath as I plunge beneath the surface. It forces the air from my body, and I try to breathe, but salty water rushes into my lungs. The cold envelops me, and I am slowly sinking deeper into the darkness. My arm and legs stiffen from the cold, and everything slows. The blue that had made the water so inviting is now gone, replaced by a dirty brown. Something sinister moves in the depths below. I flap my arms wildly trying to reach the surface, but my muscles are slow to respond, and I only seem to sink more slowly. Then, as if realizing its mistake, time speeds up to where each second blurs into the next. By some miracle, my head breaks the surface, and I cough, trying to expel the water from my lungs. Will has already begun to row back to shore. I try to swim after him, but I'm having trouble staying afloat. I try to paddle forward, but my head once again dips below the surface before I struggle back up. I yell for him to stop, but he rows faster, leaving me in the open ocean.

Chapter 35

SEARCH

The Outsiders scurry like ants in the fading light, searching for something. A group runs out of the forest and walks up to a tall dark-haired woman.

"Nothin'."

"Are ya sure?"

"Sure as can be. There're no footprints of any kind."

"OK, thanks for givin' it a shot guys."

"No prob, Chris," the ones from the forest settle to warm themselves at the fire pit as another voice speaks up.

"Chris, what's the point? I mean, why do ya care?"

"Shut up, Will."

His face gets red, and he says, "How do ya know that kid didn't go back to the Collective to tell 'em about us? We should move. I mean, they could be coming right now."

"Oh my god, Will, shut up! I'm tryin' to think."

"Are ya even listening to what I'm sayin'?"

She ignores him.

"Fine. I was just tryin' to help, but never mind," and Will sulks back into the shadows of a building.

Chapter 36

FOUND

I pry my frozen fingers off the driftwood I've been clinging to. I can't feel my hands or feet as I pull myself out of the freezing water, dragging my unresponsive body onto the sand. My limbs barely respond, but I jerk them out of the waves with the last of my strength. I had been shaking until recently, but now my muscles seem too tired to even do that. I see the small camp not far away. I try to call to the people I know must be there, but the salt water has stripped my voice. All I can manage is a horse whisper. "Help, help, h-h," then I go into a coughing fit. Shivers ripple through me, jarring and painful, but my brain is in a fog, making it impossible to think. I focus on the throbbing in my fingers, trying to stay awake. If I fall asleep, I might never wake up. I lie huddled on the cold sand until the first rays of sun come over the edge of the sea.

Soon, soon they will wake; soon they will find me lying here and, hopefully, help me. As long as it's not Will who finds me. I don't know what he would do seeing me here. Probably kill me, slit my throat, then say he found me like this, or maybe he would put me back in a boat and leave me to the sea again. I would have no strength to stop him.

I hear a shriek, then yelling. "Chris, Chris, come quick!" I hear hurried footsteps then, "Oh my. Go run and bring Ella." Then to me, "hang on, hang on."

"Hope, help me lift." I feel myself being lifted and carried with shuffling steps to sit by a warm fire. The shivering becomes violent and the pain in my fingers and toes becomes unbearable as they throb in the sudden warmth. Then a cloth is wrapped around my shoulders and a calm soft voice tells me what to do, "Drink this." I drink, spilling some of the warm beverage down my shirt as my teeth chatter. "Can ya squeeze my hand?" I do and then hear, "Can ya raise yur foot?" I struggle to raise my leg. "Is that the highest ya can raise it?" It is, and I nod. "OK, that's fine." Then walking away and whispering.

I sit, not entirely caring what they are saying. I watch the dancing flames and listen to the crackle of the fire. It seems everyone is leaving me be, and I am fine with that. The shaking slows to a slight tremor and the throbbing dulls in my fingers and toes. I raise them to my face and see that they are caked in sand. I lower my arm, not having enough strength to brush it off. The flames blur before my eyes, and I drift off in a dreamless sleep. A question drags me back from my slumber.

"Can ya tell us what happened?" asks Chris.

I look up into her concerned eyes and nod. They all sit or stand huddled around me. I hesitate before saying, "after Will and I went fishing, I went back to look at the water. I fell in, and the waves pulled me away. I'm not really sure how I managed to get back." I feel everyone's eyes on me, but I don't say anything else, just determinedly stare into the flames.

"Well, yu'll recover. It may take a bit, but yu'll be fine," says a person I assume is a healer of some sort. "Ya can move your fingers and toes now. None'll fall off."

"Thank you," I say but don't look up.

As people slowly leave, a plate is pushed into my hands, and I look up wanting to thank the person. All I see are Will's quizzical eyes. He whispers "Why, why'd ya say that?"

I pause. "You were only trying to protect them," I say, gesturing to the others. "You were being selfless. I can understand that, but I promise you that I am not trying to harm any of you. You don't need to see me as a danger, and I can leave if you wish."

He looks at me with utter bewilderment before mumbling, "no, ya don't need to do that. And—and sorry," then quickly walks away.

Chapter 37

HOLIDAY

It's been a few weeks since I found these Outsiders, and Chris has been allowing me to be a protégé of sorts. I help advise her on the Collective's tactics and devise strategies and plans in case the Collective finds this camp. I think Chris has figured out that I wasn't very forthcoming about my position in the Collective, but thankfully, she doesn't say anything. Over the past few days, people have mostly been politely cordial, but I have caught many staring at me when they thought I wasn't looking.

I'm in a meeting with Chris and the others in the village. I told Chris about how the Collective made raiding plans, so she's been reworking their entire strategy. I play with the sand beneath my feet, digging my toes deep into the fine sand before slowly lifting them up, letting the sand slide off. I could pay attention to the meeting, but the feeling of the sand on my bare feet is much more appealing than their bland conversation.

From the little I've heard, there is a large signal fire that is to be lit in the event the Collective comes. They have been reworking their entire job system too. Before, most of the village would leave and do one thing together. Now groups are split up so if an ambush occurs, the majority will be able to escape. I try to point out that this whole plan hinges on a raid occurring during the day, there not being any rain, someone being able to light the fire, and someone noticing the fire. No one hears me as I say this, however, because they are all loudly arguing over who gets the next serving of fish. That is one of the things the Collective is better at. The Collective made absolutely sure that everyone was done with the current topic before moving on. Here you just kind of shout until someone listens. I am still growing accustomed to the ways of the Outsiders. The stark contrast to the Collective can be jarring at times.

The meeting ends when someone suggests they all need to get ready for the coming days. Everyone seems pleased with this and disperses. I'm not sure how the next week is meant to be any different from the past few days, but I have noticed an excitement building among the Outsiders. After the meeting is over, I jog to catch up with Chris, but she's still busy. I wait for a minute, Chris doesn't pause in her conversation. Instead, I ask Will.

"Huh. Didn't ya have holidays in the Collective?" He asks.

"What is a holiday?"

"Uhh, it's like a party" He sees my blank expression and tries again. "A party is when a lot of people hang out and have fun together."

"Oh." I don't understand how a party is different than every day when the Outsiders gather and eat together.

I think Will senses my confusion because he continues saying,"It's, well, it's also more than that. It's a feelin', a thought. It's everyone coming together to do somethin' special. It's something to look forward to when everything seems so distant. It's light in the darkness. It's a thousand memories combining into one single feeling that fills ya up until you can't help but smile." He pauses and seems to be watching something. A forgotten memory, perhaps, a fleeting image crossing his mind. Then it's gone, and his brow furrows again, and the corners of his lips turn back down into his familiar sullen expression.

"Hey, kid, come're," says Chris. "Kid" is what all of the Outsiders have decided to call me, even though I am many years older than the majority of the children. I don't think they mean to belittle me. When the Outsiders found out who my mother supposedly was, there had been a huge shift in their attitude. "Kid" seems to be their way of acknowledging who I am.

I walk over to Chris. She's finished her conversation and is now trying to arrange the storage of food. She doesn't look up from what she's doing as she asks, "Did ya need somethin'?"

"I was just wondering what a holiday is. Everyone's really excited about it. But Will explained it to me."

"Oh, sorry." Chris looks up at me now, "I forgot, y'all don't celebrate anythin' in the Collective, do ya."

"No, they don't."

"Right, right. It gets kind of complicated, but I'll make sure to come by every day or send someone to make sure ya know what's going on—I'm pretty busy, ya see. It gets dark here so early this time of year, and there's still so much to do, but at least it ain't snow'n." I want to ask what snow is, but I don't think it's the right time.

"Okay, that's fine," I say. "Do you need help with anything?"

"Ya, some help would be great actually." She scribbles on a little piece of paper and hands it to me. "Can ya just handle this for me while I go see to the wood gatherin'?" I take the paper from her and nod. She smiles briefly and then yells for someone across the village in true Chris fashion.

I look down at the paper. It has instructions for overseeing the storage of a few kinds of grains and root vegetables. The Outsiders keep these sorts of things in little caves they call "cellars," and each has to be put away in a particular way to keep them from getting eaten by pests or rotten from dampness and mold. I walk to the first cellar to examine the progress so far. Some of those who were tasked with food storage had stopped working when Chris left and were joking around when I arrive.

Once they see me looking at them, they hurriedly start to work again.

There is excitement in the air. Unfortunately, this tends to make people sloppy rather than driven, and as people begin to leave, I discover that several bags of food need to be re-sorted and stored differently. I get to work as the cellars get quieter and the circle around the fire gets louder. Soon, just Will and I are left to finish the project on our own. I stand, lifting a moderately heavy bag filled with grain, and lug it into a small hut so that it can remain dry. Will takes the last one and then shuts the door to the cellar before we return to the center of the camp to sit around the fire with the others. I look around and notice some of my former coworkers eating and avoiding eye contact with Will or me. Will gestures to one who seems to be hiding behind a stump to avoid my gaze. Will looks at me, grinning, and I smile back. The rest of our meal is sprinkled with laughter as we continue noticing people who are desperate to avoid meeting our eyes.

Chapter 38

UNITY

I wake to the sound of excited voices and children shrieking and running around. I sit up and rub my shoulders. Between the hard bed and lifting the heavy food yesterday, my neck and shoulder seem to be made of cement. Chris knocks on the door and says, "Today is the first of the holidays. Today we celebrate unity. The kids make winter flower crowns, and songs are sung to keep the bad spirits at bay and welcome the good ones! Have fun!" She disappears back into the village. I get up and walk out the door. It is a crisp cool morning with a bright blue sky and a soft breeze blowing the tall grass. The kids are whizzing around the camp holding large bundles of grass and flowers which they bring to the older kids who carefully weave them into ornate circlets. I walk to the center of the village and see a large log in the fire pit. Chris had told me that the log burns the whole week to help commemorate the holiday, so it has to be very large. Many people are sitting around it sipping a hot brown liquid. When I sit, someone passes a cup to me, and I smell it curiously. It's warm and kind of woody with an unexpected crispness.

"It's called coffee," says the woman sitting adjacent to me. "It's a tradition to drink it on the first day." I raise it to my lips and take a sip. I try to swallow, but the taste reminds me of dirt and makes me gag. I try to seem as if I am enjoying it, but apparently I'm unsuccessful. The woman laughs, "It's fine if ya don't like it; few do. Yur mother hated it and couldn't stand the taste. I was curious if ya were the same."

"Oh," I laugh. She takes the cup and pours my coffee into her mug. My mother . . . the Outsiders often say things like this, small bits of information that they retained throughout the long years. Only a few here actually knew her, I think, but they all pretend that they did. I settle down on the sand that has been warmed by the fire and prop my head on a log to watch the clouds lazily float by in the sky and feel the breeze tussle my hair. The children have begun to squabble about the correct way to weave flower crowns. An adult rushes towards them and breaks up the argument. Laughter floats on the breeze as I drift into sleep.

•—•—•

A poke in my ribs wakes me. A small child is standing in front of me holding a circlet of woven flowers and grass. "For me?" I ask. She nods and pushes it into my hands. She herself has little white winter flowers adoring her head. "Thank you," I say gently, and she smiles and nods before running off. I hold the circlet in my hand. The flowers have been interlaced with the green ivy and tall grasses that grow in abundance around the camp. I delicately place it on my head, not wanting to disturb the careful work.

I walk over to where the others are gathered. Some of the children pull me away and start trying to teach me something. I try to mimic their rhythmic chanting and rhyming lines, but they laugh and make odd warbling sounds with their voices like birds. A low humming starts emanating from those standing around the fire. It grows louder, and the kids run towards the sound. That's when I realize: this is singing. I've never sung before—music didn't really exist in the Collective—and I catch my breath as I finally understand what the children were trying to teach me. The soft melody flows through the air and, as more voices join, it grows louder. The song reverberates on the water, which sends back the sound again, distorted. The haunting melody becomes one with the breeze and floats around the camp. There are no discernible words, but the message is clear. It is a sound of joy, of hope. It pushes the darkness back and seems to glow with unseen light. It's a light that starts from within, warming every inch of my body down to my toes, where it radiates out, becoming one invisible warmth. The fire flickers and grows, seeming to be fed by the song. As it had started, the song slowly turns to a low hum, then stops, sending shivers up my spine. However, the darkness does not return. The light from the song stays even though the singing has ceased.

Chapter 39

THE RACE

"Go, Jay!" A lady sitting adjacent to me cheers. A young man who must be Jay comes around the corner, running towards the finish line. Chris had woken me up this morning with an exuberant energy that is echoed by the rest of the Outsiders. The cheering and yells echo around me as others see Jay. I'm still not really used to falling asleep and waking up naturally, and it's too early for this much enthusiasm. Suddenly Will sprints around the same corner. In no time, Will is even with Jay. Now both Jay and Will are running full tilt towards the finish line. The crowd is going crazy as the two come within feet of the finish line. The thin string spanning the length of the finish line is broken, and everyone is asking one another, "Wait, who won?" Jay and Will sit on a grassy hill gasping for breath. The remainder of the racers finish, a few straggling several minutes behind Will and Jay.

Chris gets everyone's attention before saying, "As many of y'all saw, the first place is a tossup. The string that's suppose' to help up in such a situation came loose on the side that Will finished, so we've decided that," she pauses in anticipation before saying, "It is a tie! Congratulations Jay and Will!" The crowd erupts into cheering and many go to congratulate Will and Jay on their victory. Jay flashes a winning smile, and thanks all his congratulators before walking over to Will, who is sulking in the corner. Jay offers his hand to Will in a sign of good sportsmanship. Startled, Will shakes it, and another round of cheering bursts out. Jay's admirers accompany him back to camp, and I wait for Will.

"You did really well."

"Thanks. Not like it was worth anything. That self-righteous idiot won anyway. Did ya see the way he shook my hand? It was all for show," he says sourly.

I nod my head, knowing that it is not the best idea to say more on this subject. "For the record, I don't think it was a tie," I say, and the scowl on his face lessens.

We walk the rest of the way to camp in silence. As we near the center of camp, a scowl returns to Will's face. Jay has decided to ignore the fact that the race has been deemed a tie and is giving those around him a play by play of his "victory." Will sits in the corner of the camp, as far away as he can get from Jay. I can tell he feels unappreciated, as he so often does, so I sit with him as I listen to his ranting about the unfairness of every-thing. I occasionally chime in a, "ya," or an, "mmm."

Competitions continue throughout the day, as the holiday's theme is determination. There are more races of various sorts, but also games for the mind and tests of strength. I participate in some of the strategic games, but stay clear of the competitions that require physical endurance. As time passes, I start to notice that Jay has been trying to catch my eye. I ignore him, not amused by the way he treated Will, but he is persistent. He joins the games I play, even though he always loses, and tries to make conversation. I focus on the games, and as a result, I win all of them. Many of the Outsiders don't have much of an eye for strategy. Many years ago in the Collective, there were strategy games that everyone would be encouraged to play, but then everyone became too adept at them, and they were retired to be used in the school. As the end of the day is nearing, I finish a game of "Mancala" with a middle aged woman. After the game is over, she congratulates me, and I thank her for playing with me. She smiles and nods before walking into the center of camp to talk with some of her friends. I also walk into camp, but I'm stopped by a hand on my shoulder. It makes me jump and I look around quickly to see Jay standing there.

"Umm, do you need something?" I ask, trying to sound polite.

"Errr, ya, ya wanna go for a walk or something?"

"No, I'm good. I'm going to have dinner."

"Well, OK." He frowns. I start to walk towards the camp but he calls out again saying "Ya know I won the race earlier today, and Will lost, and ya haven't con-gratulated me yet. And it's, uhh, kinda rude."

"You didn't win the race. You tied," I say shortly. He looks genuinely confused at this.

"Uhh, I don't know what yu're talking about. Everyone saw me win. Everyone has been saying it all day. No one thinks he won be-because I won," he finishes smugly.

"What's taking so long?" Will asks as he ap-proaches us.

"Oh, nothing, Will, we were just talking about how I won the race," Jay needles.

"No, neither of you two won, and you both need to stop behaving like childish idiots." I retort. Will looks like he wants to say something, but I push past him, and he quietly follows me toward the fire.

"Ya know, pretending to be Will's friend isn't going to help. He is useless. Everyone knows it." Jay yells after us.

"Don't," I say to Will as my friend tenses to turn around. "That's what he wants." I can't believe how childish the people here can be. Jay is just immature enough to need gratification from every single person, regardless of the hurt it can cause. We walk into camp where Will and Jay spend the rest of the evening glaring at one another from their respective "thrones," which are more like chairs with pillows stuck to the back. Apparently, the race's winner gets the privilege of presiding over the meal, and even though Jay argues with Chris that he won, she insists that the two of them share this duty. Jay announces when we begin eating, and Will gets to decide when we stop. I think that this is a weird way to show respect, but it is not my place to question their traditions.

This dinner is much more tense than previous ones have been. Others have noticed that Will and Jay are glaring at each other, but no one says anything. As soon as Will declares that dinner is over, I go to my hut and do my best to fall asleep, not wanting to talk to anyone.

Chapter 40

THE PLATFORM

I blink my eyes in the bright morning light that's spilling through my doorway past Chris's shoulders and beaming directly into my face. Sleep hadn't come easily to me last night, and I'm barely awake now. I need to wake myself up, though, because Chris is now explaining to me what we're doing today.

"OK, so, today is the third day, and it's about community achievements. Basically, I decide on a project that I think'd be helpful to have. For example, those boats were a project about ten-ish years ago, and some of the huts were projects too. I decided that this year we're going to build a lookout platform. After ya told us all about the Collective's strategies, I've been toying with this idea, and I think it'd be helpful, and at least it'll be a cool view, ya know."

"OK, what do you need me to do?"

"Well, everyone's already up and working on it. If you could help with the ladder, that'd be great." She leaves, and I groan as I get up.

Everyone is gathered in the center of town and wrapped in blankets against the biting wind, trying to stay awake. I guess "working on it" was a bit of an exaggeration. A group of people are picking out tools and are getting ready to go into the woods, presumably to get wood or pick out a tree. The rest seem to be trying to make a ladder, but they are extraordinarily disorganized. A rope lies knotted around a set of boards while another is strung through a series of holes in a larger plank. Pieces of wood and tools are scattered everywhere, and several groups of people are arguing over various tasks while others huddle off to the side avoiding getting involved. I walk over to a grumbling group. The sand is being swept up by a breeze, and fine grit pelts my face. I squint and clear my throat trying to get their attention.

They ignore me. I cough again, more loudly, and some look up for a moment.

"Who's in charge here?" I ask.

"Me." I spin around and see Jay flashing his infuriatingly pompous smile as he throws some boards onto the ground.

"Well, do you have a plan?"

"Well, duh."

"Really?"

"...No."

"That's what I thought. You two, grab those ropes and set them parallel to each other," I say pointing at two sitting in the sand. "The rest of you take a plank and use the hand drills to make a hole on each end that the rope can fit through. Start on this end and thread your board up both the ropes, then tie a large knot underneath it on each side two hand-lengths from the knot above. Everyone got it?" There's a scuffling as everyone starts doing what I told them.

"What do you think you are doing?" says Jay indignantly.

"What you can't," I say.

In no time, we finish the ladder. Someone comes to show us the selected tree, and we carry the ladder into the woods. The other group has been gathering wood for the structure. Sophie, who is small and nimble, scurries up the tree with the ladder. She deftly leaps from limb to limb, swinging herself up onto higher branches. Once she finds a satisfactory spot, she secures the ladder to the tree and lets it fall. It's a bit longer than necessary, and several boards clatter on the ground. Sophie presses one foot, then her whole body onto it to test it with her weight. It holds, and she climbs down the ladder, jumping the last few feet to the bottom.

She gives a thumbs up and says, "I found a good spot, but there are a few branches that need to be cut."

A few others busy themselves by securing the ladder to the ground before grabbing boards and climbing to the top. One carries a small saw in her teeth as she climbs up the ladder. I sit, leaning against a neighboring tree, and watch the platform being built. A few others are sitting nearby, but I feel no need to talk to them. I am content to watch the platform slowly forming high in the tree. Once the landing is built, branches are positioned over the platform to disguise it. It's not long until the platform is completely concealed and the workers climb down the ladder.

I've never had much of a problem with heights, however, I am not eager to go up onto the platform. Chris is urging me to climb, saying that the view is awesome. I don't care how "awesome" it is. I don't want to go up. However, I can tell she is very proud of the project, so I begrudgingly get up and start to climb. Even though it's been secured to the ground, the ladder is still wobbly and shakes as I climb. Or maybe I'm the one who's shaking. As I climb higher and higher into the tree, I am making a concerted effort to only watch my hands moving up the ropes and to not look down. I am glad I had taken the time to set each wood piece equidistant to one another. My hands feel raw from gripping the rope. I hit my head on the platform and raise my arm, searching for something solid to grip so I can pull myself up. I grab a branch and hoist myself onto the platform and breathing heavily, I look at the green canopy above. I lie there until Chris gets to the top, then I sit up and immediately regret it. The small platform has no walls or even a rope around it, and it rocks in the wind, swaying with the branches. It feels too small for the two of us. Chris, however, seems like she is at home high above the ground. She sits on the edge of the platform, letting her legs dangle lazily off the edge.

"Aren't you going to put any rails or some sort of precaution to keep people from falling?" I say. Chris contemplates the idea of safety rails. I don't think she sees how dangerous it is to be up here, let alone without anything to prevent someone from falling.

"Oh stop bein' such a chicken."

"Chicken" is a term that the Outsiders use to convince one another to do stupid things. I don't get it. Chris sighs, resigning herself to the fact that I am not moving any closer to the edge. I am firmly planted next to the trunk. The view is beautiful. The platform is pointed away from the sea towards miles and miles of trees that dance in the wind. A bird soars in the sky with a fish in its claws and flaps its giant wings before disappearing into the clouds.

"You know who I am don't you," I say, not really asking.

She sighs before saying, "Ya, I do." I can tell she had been trying to avoid this conversation.

"Then why do you trust me? If you know what I am and what I was being trained to do."

"It's not what ya are; it's who ya want to be. That's the important bit. Yu're here. Ya left. Ya don't want to be a part of the Collective. That proves to me that yu're not all gone, there's some of ya still left. No matter how hard they tried to claw it out of ya, yur individuality is what sets ya apart from the Collective and is why I can trust ya," says Chris.

I find myself flinching at the word "individuality." To be an 'individual' in the Collective is to be selfish and therefore shameful. But here it's different. Here, it's not what I am, it's what I want to be. I don't want to be a part of the Collective. I guess she's right—as long as I hang on to myself I will never be a part of the Collective.

"Ya wanna see somethin' cool?"

"Sure," I say, startled out of my trance.

"See that knot on that tree?" She's pointing to a cedar about sixty feet away. She opens her jacket and reveals a long row of knives. She carefully selects one of the glistening blades and balances it in her hand. She tosses it up before saying "watch this," and it soars toward the knot. In seconds a 'twange' signifies that the knife has found its mark. I squint and see the knife in the dead center of the knot.

"Cool, right?" she says. "I've been knife throwin' for as long as I can remember."

"How far can you throw it?" I ask.

"Uhhh, I think my best was 98 feet."

I look at her, shocked, "What? And you hit your mark every time?"

"Nearly, ya. The further it is, the harder it is to aim. 98 feet is the farthest I threw it when hittin' the bullseye. I can actually throw farther, but it doesn't really count."

"Whoa," I say as she lazily spins a knife on her finger before saying, "it's probably time to head down." I agree, and we begin the slow descent to the ground. She goes first and reaches the ground long before I do. Going down is much more difficult than I had expected. I lower my foot on to the next rung, but it slips, leaving my leg dangling in empty space. I kick it around trying to find the rung. Involuntarily, I look down. I see Chris, the size of an ant, standing below. I clutch the ladder breathing heavily, and my brain reels with the prospect of dropping to the ground. My hands were shaking as on the assent, but it's much worse now. My foot finally touches the ground, and I find Chris waiting for me.

"Fun, right!" She says enthusiastically.

"Yeah," I say, grimacing, my heart still banging on my rib cage, trying to escape.

Chapter 41

BROKEN

Will, Chris, Ella, and I are the only ones left sitting around the fire. The embers glow, and sparks shoot up into the sky. "So, ya still haven't told us how ya got out of the Collective," Will grunts.

"Well, I just kind of...left. It was easy."

"Really? We've always had trouble getting people out," Chris says.

"Strange," I say. "It was really simple. Everyone just ignored me. I still don't know how I came here though."

"Well, you just kinda showed up on the beach near one of the rivers nearby. You were ice cold, and the ones who found ya thought ya were dead. Ella here said it was worth the shot to try to save ya."

"Good thing she did," I laugh. Ella shrugs her shoulders, not saying anything. She tends to talk little, seeming to think that words are precious and should not be wasted. Chris stands and brushes off her pants before going to bed. Will shortly follows, and it's just Ella and me sitting by the flickering fire. She stands up to go to bed, but before she does, she turns to me saying, "The back of your neck has been flashing. I don't think anyone else noticed. Thought you should know." Then, without saying another word, she leaves.

The crackling fire fills the silence as I sit thinking about what that might mean. The rock in the river must have broken my chip when I smashed into it, and the light is the chip shutting down. Tentatively, I try to reach around to feel the back of my neck. I can feel what seems to be my chip, but there are multiple hard lumps below the surface of my skin. It's broken; my last connection to the Collective has been severed, cut.

Chapter 42

DAY OF PURPOSE

Yesterday was the day of responsibility. When Chris had described it to me as a day for telling people how you really feel about them, I thought that it would be a day of selflessly exposing the truth while being unafraid of the hurt it might cause. That couldn't have been further from the truth. Throughout the day, many people expressed how much they valued one another, but no one said anything really negative. Many chose to avoid hurting anyone's feelings by simply telling everyone that they were valued, even if it couldn't possibly be true. Others told no one, choosing only to enjoy the praise they got from others. Only a few used the day as it was intended, seeking out specific people and communicating true feelings.

Yesterday stands in stark contrast to today, the day of purpose, in which people focus on themselves. For those who already do this, it makes them insufferable. They spend the day recounting their great deeds. A few do reflect on their purpose, what they are here to do and what they can do with the time that they have. In short, some have an existential crisis when they can't find any purpose in their lives. The rest, who know that they have a purpose and are confident that they are doing something with their life, avoid this rabbit hole, knowing it will ultimately lead them nowhere. Those of us who choose not to engage in either of these options have to watch the conflicting waves of overconfidence and mental breakdowns. I think it's very amusing watching one person talking about what a gift to humanity he is while another is hysterically crying. Will, however, has been trying to help those who are having a hard time. He showed me how to put together little baskets with blankets, water and food so he could go hand them out to the distraught people, but I haven't made as many as he would have liked. He comes back after a couple of hours and looks disappointed when he sees the dearth of baskets.

"Sorry, I have a lot on my mind," I say sheepishly.

He relents and says, "It's alright," before scooping up the few baskets in the sand next to me and walking over to yet another person who cries softly under the clamor of Jay crowing about himself.

•—•—•

It has been rather hard to sleep with sobs coming intermittently throughout the night. A small group of people around my age have gathered by the fire to watch the stars. I listen to them crack jokes while I lie on the cooling sand, feeling the heat dissipate into the brisk night air. I doze off in the cool sand for a bit before I am awakened by another round of sobbing from a hut nearby. Others around me rise and brush themselves off before walking into the woods. I decide to follow, not wanting to be left alone and knowing that I'm not going to get any sleep tonight. One of them spins around, bumping into trees while singing a cheery song about dandelions. Others join in, and they laugh hysterically when one of them rams into a tree trunk with a resounding thud that sends pine needles cascading down on top of their heads. The one who started the song laughs and spins in the falling debris.

"Hope, come on," laughs a guy. She has fallen behind a bit as she spins in the pine needles. Hope skips up to the rest of the group.

"What's the hurry Benny boo? No one will notice we are gone until the sun comes up," says Hope. His friends laugh.

"Benny boo, ooooo," says one.

"So how long has it been 'Benny boo' for?" another says very seriously.

"Ya, Benny boo, how come ya didn't tell us?" another says similarly serious.

"Shut up," says Ben, the redness of his face illuminated by the moon. Uproarious laughter erupts from his friends as they notice his flushed face. In no time, we reach the tree where the platform rests, and I see them coming up with a very stupid idea. They plan to climb the ladder in the middle of the night and do what? Look at the stars? It's easily enough to do that from the ground. They start the climb to the top anyway. I grapple with the prospect of climbing after them, decide I should, put my foot on the first rung, and then decide not to. Well, actually, *I* don't decide, my stomach does. I look up and see the last of the group disappearing onto the platform. They don't care enough to wait for me or check if I'm coming after them.

I turn and start to walk back to the camp when a scream echoes through the night. It's different from the ones earlier. This scream is not of sadness or despair, but of terror. It echoes through the darkness, making my heart drop. It happened: someone fell off the platform. I run back to the tree and see Hope lying next to the ladder. Dead.

Chapter 43

WON'T

She lies on the ground, her braided hair stuck to her face and a bullet hole showing clean through the center of her forehead. Blood is soaking into the soil around her, staining her blond hair crimson. The shot went straight through her brain. I only know a few who can aim like this, a few who have the tools to do this.

The Collective.

My heart pounds with the realization as it sets in. I don't know how they could have found me. I look to the water, tantalizingly close, then towards camp. If I go to the water, I can escape along the coastline and save myself, but surely the soldiers will find everyone else and kill them. I sprint to the large pile of dry tinder for the warning fire that Chris and I had set up and scrape one of the precious matches to light it. It ignites instantly, sending a pillar of flames high into the sky, illuminating everything around. Something cracks in the woods, and I leap into a sprint. Not towards the water, but towards camp. As I reach the first huts, I bang on the doors and shout,"The Collective! Run!"

Chris stumbles out of her hut and sleepily says "Huh." I grab her arms and shake her before saying, "The Collective. They are here. We need to go. Hope is dead! We need to leave," I yell. "Untie the boats."

No one moves, so I shout "Go, GO!" In an instant, the mood changes from sleepy annoyance to a frenzy. Many are sprinting to the boats, parents running back into huts to grab children, and a few help me to knock on doors. The boats have been flipped and pushed into the water when zips fill the air. People dive behind huts, and more screams fill the air as people drop where they stand. There are a few remaining who don't know any of this is happening.

The shots are coming from the right. If I run diagonally, I can reach the furthest huts. I glance behind me to see that no one else is still trying to knock on the remaining doors; those who were helping me must have left for the boats with everyone else as soon as shots were fired. I alone can get to them. I duck behind the edge of a neighboring hut and sprint, bent over, to the huts, pounding on the doors. "The Collective is here. Follow me," I yell. Once all the huts are emptied, the frightened individuals run behind me as I weave in and out of huts. I turn in time to see two more drop, leaving me and three others. I started with ten. I look back to see if anyone is still there and hot thick blood sprays over my face. Two.

The boats are about to push off. I tell the last two following me to go in front. They do, and we run towards the boats. Slipping on the mixture of sand and blood, I hear a whizzing and duck, pulling the closest person down with me. She teeters for a moment before collapsing into the sand. They got her neck. She lies there, slowly drowning in her own blood.

I push the last person towards the boats and turn back to the woman. Her hand shakily moves to her neck and tries to staunch the bleeding. I already know that it will do no good. She's all but dead now. I fumble in the sand, and my hand closes around a fragment of glass. I flinch as the sharp edge bites into my fingers, but I seize the shard and place it in the woman's hand. She looks at me, and I see understanding and gratitude in her eyes as she slides her hand with the glass along her neck, cutting a jagged line deep into the skin. Her last breath leaves her, and the shard of glass falls into the sand. No one should have to suffer like that.

I look out to the water and see the boats already disappearing into the blackness. No, no, no. I see Will, Chris and Jay on the closest boat. Something is wrong. The boats are still moving away. I squint and see Jay holding Will around the middle as he's throwing himself at Chris, screaming at her. She pretends not to hear.

I sprint to the shore, preparing to swim out to meet them. I splash into the water and run until my shoulders are just above the surface. Then I dive under the water, and salt stings my eyes just as a cold hand closes around my ankle and pulls me backward. I kick my leg, trying to free myself from the grasp, but it only closes tighter. Then another and another, pulling me onto the sand. Pulling me away from freedom. I scream and silent bubbles float to the surface. My face is being dragged on the rocks and sand. It breaks the surface and I gasp for air. I am pushed to my knees, facing the water. They grind my legs into the sand and shove my shoulders to get me to lie prone, but I push against them. I look out onto the water and see the moonlight glint on something. Chris. She's wearing her knife vest. I look at her and scream, "Please, Chris, please do it." I've seen her hit targets from an even greater distance. She looks at me. Our eyes meet. She knows what I want her to do. I close my eyes waiting for it to end, but nothing happens, only more people trying to force me to the ground. I try to stay upright, to give her a better target, but it still doesn't come. I look up and see her turn away.

Will is screaming at her, and I hear him begging her to do it. But she does not end my suffering. She won't do it. How was I so foolish? I give up, let myself be slammed into the sand. Chris, who valued my ideas and knowledge, who seemingly took a fondness to me, she won't do it. She would not end my suffering. For I will suffer. They will make certain of this. My hands and legs are restrained. It's not necessary. I won't fight. They've won.

Chapter 44

AGAIN

I open my eyes and see a bright white surrounding me. Confused, I blink, and the room comes into focus. I am in a room made of glowing light. I try to look around to the other side of the chamber, but my head has a thick strap securing it to the chair. Then it strikes me—this is where I had my chip implanted. I try to free my hands, but they are secured with the same straps. No one bothered filing down the sharp points of the cold metal chair, and the two bars supporting my head are digging into my skin. I hear the sound of a door slowly opening behind me, and I wait for whoever just entered to come into my field of view.

A sigh comes from behind me, and Charles says, "You were so close. I thought this would be your last time, but Mallory messed it all up with her radical thinking. You were supposed to find the information in a controlled environment where I could explain to you why and you could fully understand the reasons behind it. I'm sorry about that. We shouldn't have let you get that attached to her. One of the things that makes the system successful is the lack of connections. We kept you mostly isolated in your youth, except for Alex, but he was always going to be cut. He never lost that..." he pauses, looking for the right word, "Outsider charm." He then laughs, saying, "But you, you did! I'll admit you did a better job than normal evading our search. Most of the time you just do the same thing over and over, but we have to let you out in order to track your progress. Being on the outside makes you take selfish actions; how easily you take those actions tells us how far you have come. Normally we let you wander until you get into trouble or find some Outsiders so we can round them up with you. This time, however, you spent an abnormally long time with them. Sorry about that, they are so… dirty. I—"

"Why?" I interrupt. My head is spinning. Answers to subconscious questions are clicking into place, and I'm not liking the result.

Surprised Charles retorts, saying, "What do you mean, 'Why'?"

"Why all this?"

"You need to lose your empathy; we need you to be selfish. Ironic, I know," he says. The ominous sound of heels tapping on the hard floor signifies Elisabeth's arrival. I try to turn to look at her, but remember that I'm bound, completely motionless, to my chair. Her cold voice echoes in the sanitized space.

"You can go now, Charles. You have said your goodbyes, and after all, it's not for long," she says.

He dutifully leaves, shutting the door behind him. Now it's just Elisabeth standing ominously behind my chair.

"Selflessness is vital to maintain order in the Collective; however, to be a leader, you need to be selfish. Without it, you will never be able to exert absolute power over others. You cannot think about them as unique people. You must only know them as part of the Collective, and you must work for the betterment of the Collective, no matter the pain it causes. In order to do this, you must lose your empathy. It is a long process, but once it is done, you can finally step into the role of leader," she says in a rehearsed voice.

I try to ask for clarification, but she continues, as if anticipating my question, "For instance, Mallory, she had many chances to lose her empathy, but it always remained. But you, you have such promise! I was so disappointed when we had to let you out again. You may not understand the necessity of these actions yet, but you will soon."

"I know more now than I ever learned with you," I sputter angrily.

She finally comes around the chair so I can see her. Her face is stiff, but there's a hint of pity in her eyes, "They really messed you up, but don't worry. Soon you won't remember any of this. You get what so many people long for, a fresh start!"

"I don't want a fresh start," I say, beginning to understand why I am strapped down.

"But all the pain, all the hurt will disappear! Do you know how many people would love to have a chance like that?" she says, mildly confused.

"I want to keep my memories," I say defiantly.

She smiles, "There's that self-preservation we love. Don't worry. We've all done it countless times. It's what made us such good leaders."

I try to turn to her, "You mean, you've all been through this before."

"Yes, and so have you."

"So, you've been orchestrating this from the beginning?"

"You've finally got it! We have. Well, the instance in the showers was, um, more aggressive than we planned. Your real classmates are carrying out their Assignments elsewhere and are starting to look too old for that kind of thing. These were a mix of the new generation who had received a poor Assignment and a few leftovers who suited the role. Of course, your chip's malfunction was the big surprise. That was out of our control," she admits.

I remember that rock in the river.

"Everything has been a test to try to cultivate different aspects of your selfishness. We obviously have some work yet to do—Oswald says that you helped the Outsiders to escape when you could have just run away. But we'll get there. As soon as you can understand the actions that need to be taken, you can join us, but not yet." She looks at me with an air of finality before pausing and saying, "Good luck."

She turns to leave. I plead with her to not do it, but she ignores me and walks out of the room. Someone enters and presses a cold cylinder into the back of my neck. I desperately pull at my restraints, wanting to make them stop, to somehow knock it out of their hands and flee.

It's no use. The straps hold strong. I feel a slight burning sensation starting where the cylinder is in contact with my skin, and it grows until it is nearly unbearable, flooding the rest of my body, leaving it numb. Numb. I don't want to be numb again. I cry out, begging for them to make it stop. I don't want to forget. I don't want to start over. I yell and scream, trying to save myself, the "me" that I have become. I lie. I tell them that I can change, that I don't need to start over, that I understand now, and other nonsensical blather. I don't want to restart. I don't want to forget. My body convulses, fighting against the inevitable. Tears stream down my face.

Chapter 45

NOTHING

Then, nothing.

"I'm sorry that had to happen, but we almost lost you," says Elisabeth. The attendant undoes the straps, freeing me from the metal frame. "Anyway, welcome back."

Made in the USA
Coppell, TX
20 July 2021

59232601R00100